Tom's Town

James J. Stewart

ISBN: 978-0-9861334-3-5

Other books by James J. Stewart available at

Amazon.com and CreateSpace.com:

Gaardian Tales
Life Before Conception
Starlight Adventures
The Still Small Voice
Stepping Beyond
The Gaardian Saga [The four above in one volume]

Poetry and Inspiration
Faith and Yosemite [Christian poetry with pictures]
Faith Fuel
Lasting Love
Walking in Faith

Yosemite Picture Books
Ever-Changing Yosemite Valley
Faith and Yosemite [see above]
Portraits of El Capitan
Portraits of Half Dome
Starlight Over Yosemite

1.

Towne was Tom's town. Tom Kuster had been the Police Chief of Towne since the previous Chief, Tony Lamprecht, had been killed after he broke up a domestic dispute. Tom had been born, raised, and educated in Towne. The city simply called 'Towne' was small by most people's standards. All of its nearly fifteen hundred residents lived in single-family houses and duplexes within a ten square mile area, nestled in the Sierra Nevada foothills. Tom thought of Towne as *his* town not only because he had been born there, but because he and his three deputies were the law for both Towne and all the ranches and farms in the county. Towne was the county seat, so Tom functioned as the County Sheriff as well as the Police Chief.

When he came into the Police Station that Monday morning at sunrise, the latest census was sitting on the corner of his desk where he had left it Saturday. The census takers had done a good job, and the data didn't surprise him. Within the official city limits, 432 were Caucasian like himself. 397 were Hispanic (including Tom's wife), 405 were African American. 47 were Native American, and the remaining 200 or so were a mix of Asians from various countries.

Tom had earned a Master of Science degree in Criminal Justice in Sacramento while a deputy in Towne, and he was brilliant. He met Maria, his future wife, while playing football as a linebacker for Towne High School. Even then, Maria was barely five feet tall, more than a foot shorter than Tom. After one game, they went out for hamburgers and shakes, and they had been together ever since.

Tom had a relatively easy calling as head of the area's law enforcement. There had not been a homicide since the death of Tony Lamprecht twenty-one years earlier, when an angry husband walked into the police station and shot him at his desk.

The town's All American Bank was robbed six years ago, but the FBI had confronted the suspects sixty miles away, and all three had died in a blaze of gunfire. Tom heard about it the evening news. In his twenty-one years as Chief, most of the crimes he and his deputies had to deal with were minor.

Tom's father, Mike Kuster, had acquired the family's land when it was cheap, right after World War II, before he got married to Tom's mother, Trina. When they retired, Mike and Tricia deeded the land over to Tom and Maria, as they moved to the San Francisco area. The insured mortgage was sizable, but it had no financial impact on their lives except for some paperwork. Each year, Tom and Maria got a mortgage bill for ten thousand dollars, to be paid a week after Tom's birthday, and each year Tom got the identical amount as a birthday gift. The gift was deposited in Tom's account, and they wrote a check to Mike and Tricia for the same amount. It was a completely legal way to avoid dealing with certain taxes.

That particular weekend, during lunch after church on Sunday, talk had not been about the worship service but about the state highway's new bridge that was almost finished. It was part of an overall widening of the highway from the Central Valley into the mountain communities like Towne. The state acquired property through eminent domain proceedings both for the bridge and the additional lanes of the highway. Tom and Maria had lost some of their land and some apple trees because of the construction, but the state was still negotiating their lawyers for the land. Tom and Maria hoped to get enough from the sale to pay off their mortgage.

That Sunday, the churches were talking together about the more businesses and residents who would come into the area with the highway's additional traffic. Towne had five churches, and there was a synagogue eleven miles west and a mosque thirty miles or so north. Tom and Maria went to all five churches once or twice a year, but most Sundays, they went to Towne Community Church, which was just a block from the county courthouse. They had done so the day before. Their five children loved going to church school on Sundays.

Now it was Monday. Tom brewed himself a large mug of Earl Grey tea, added some sugar, and lowered his 210 pounds down into the chair at his desk. Noticing the stack of Saturday's mail in his inbox, he reached for the first class letters, sitting on top of the magazines and bulk mail items. The first letter was a window envelope from the State of California. Tearing it open, on top was conventional letter printed with the state logo. After glancing through the conventional letter, he looked at the check printed underneath. The pupils of his eyes dilated. He put down his mug of tea as he stared at the check. He glanced at the letter again and then stared at the check some more. Putting it all down, he leaned back and glanced up at the clock on the wall. *Maria is fixing breakfast for the kids*, he thought. Punching the phone for a line, he picked up the receiver and dialed their number. After one ring, Maria answered, "Hello?"

"Hi, beautiful, are you busy making breakfast?"

"Hey, handsome! Of course! What's up?"

"Since you're not on duty this morning, after you drop off the kids at school, come on over to the office. We'll get some breakfast at The Little Red Hen."

"Fantastic! Steak and eggs?"

"You read my mind."

"Always! See ya!"

"Okay."

They both hung up. Tom heard the front door of the station open and close. "Jenelle?" he called out.

"Good morning, Chief! I'll be right in, after I grab a cup of coffee."

"No rush."

Soon turning forty, Tom was tall and built like a linebacker. He stayed in shape working out at the high school gym, and he was managing to keep his muscular frame from turning into fat. During football season, he helped coach the school football team. Grabbing the remaining letters, he leaned back, stretched out his long legs, put his feet up on the desk, and began to read. He could hear noises in the outer office as another deputy came in, Jack, chatting about the weekend. As Tom continued to read he heard a quiet knock on his open door. "Hey, Chief, anything in particular you want me to do today?"

Tom looked up from his reading. His best deputy, Jenelle, was tall, with flaming red hair tucked under her cap. She had been Miss Texas twelve years earlier, but had been his deputy now for more than eight years, and she was teaching martial arts at the high school one day a week. Her husband, Mike Robbins, was the Fire Chief.

Tom cocked his head and smiled. "Good morning, Jenelle! See to it that either Charly, Jack, or you patrol a little more out near the highway during daylight hours from this day forwards. I don't expect that we'll be writing many citations, but one of the construction workers was making some trouble at Bill's Bar and Grill on Saturday night. We need to have someone out there to keep an eye on things. The CHP is sending a patrol car up and down through the area more often. We're coordinating with them."

Jenelle nodded. "Okay. Mike is doing inspections at the schools. He said to give you a head up."

"Anything in particular?"

"Yeah. A couple of kids at the high school think fire safety instruction is a waste of time, or at least, they have during previous inspections. They get a bit rowdy sometimes when Mike is on campus. He can handle one or two of them, of course, but I'm still a bit concerned."

"Okay. The school is less than three blocks from the highway, so coverage won't be a problem. Right now, I'm waiting for Maria. When she and I leave for breakfast, you've got the station."

"Right." She turned and went out.

Thoughtful, Tom picked up the phone and punched in a number. "Hey, Bill, this is Chief Kuster."

"Good morning, Chief. Are you calling about Saturday night?"

"Yeah. I hear you had some trouble."

"No worries. It was manageable. A 'dozer jockey from the highway job, after having a few, got fresh with one of my waitresses. The first time she just brushed him off, but when he came back for more she decked him."

Tom laughed. "Was that Judy?"

Bill chuckled. "Yeah, Judy can handle just about anybody. She's one of Jenelle's graduates. The trouble started when getting decked just made him mad. There was a bit of a scuffle as other guys took Judy's side and tried to get the 'dozer jockey to cool off. A table was damaged and a chair broken, but by the time your deputy Charly got there a minute later, it was pretty much over. Judy told him that she did not want to press charges."

"That's what I understand. Whether or not Judy wants to press charges, if there's further trouble from any of the construction workers, I want you to call me personally. I don't want this to become routine. Okay?"

"Right, Chief, I appreciate it. ... Hold on a minute." Tom waited about two minutes, listening to some faint voices. "Tom? Judy came in to pick up her torn outfit to repair it. She wants to talk to you. Hold on."

"Okay."

Judy took the phone and spoke quietly. "Is this the Chief?"

"Yes, Judy."

"Chief, nobody got hurt except for a red place where he grabbed my rear and his sore jaw."

"I know you can take care of yourself, Judy, because Jenelle taught you well. Still, I don't want you to get hurt."

"Thanks Chief. What'll happen if there's trouble with men from that crew again?"

"We'll cross that bridge when we come to it, Judy. Meanwhile, take care of yourself."

"Okay, Chief. Bye."

"Bye, Judy." As he hung up, he looked up at the doorway.

"Hi, handsome."

"Hi, gorgeous!" He got up to greet Maria with a hug, towering over her petite frame. "Are you hungry?"

"After fixing breakfast for the kids but not eating? Are you kidding?"

Tom winked. "You can't tell me you didn't nibble a little."

Marie smiled. "Of course, but only just a little!" She put her arm through his as they went out of his office door.

"You've got the fort, Jenelle. We'll be back in an hour or so."

Jenelle nodded. "Right! Have a good breakfast!"

Tom and Maria went out the door, down the steps, and turned right towards the café. The air was still very cool, and she pulled her coat more tightly around her and leaned into him.

Maria looked up at his face. "We don't go out to breakfast very often. What's the occasion?"

"You'll see. It's a bit of a surprise." They walked silently until they got to The Little Red Hen. He held the door for her as they went in.

A waitress called out, "Hey, Chief! Hey, Maria! Take a booth! I'll be right with you! Earl Grey tea, right?"

"Right!" said Tom, and Maria nodded. After hanging up their coats on the rack just inside the door, they sat down in a booth.

They had hardly settled into their seats before Effie, the waitress, had cups of tea and an old-fashioned tea pot on their table. The waitress smiled. "I always remember you two because here's a big hunk with a petite Hispanic, who are both like Brits who love good tea."

Tom smiled. "Thanks, Effie."

"You're welcome. What'll it be?"

As Tom looked at Maria, she glanced up at Effie and said almost forcefully, "Steak, eggs over easy, and all the trimmings, medium rare!"

Tom nodded. As Effie walked away, Tom handed Maria the envelope from the State of California.

Maria unfolded the pages carefully, and started reading the letter, nodding. Then she looked at the check, and her eyes opened wide. Quietly and intensely, she said, "I didn't think our lawyer had even made headway! This is amazing!"

Tom nodded and also spoke in a low tone. "Don't you have a relative who's an investment counselor?"

"He's not a relation, but Juan Smith's been a friend for a long time. What'll we tell him?

"I'm not sure, now, with this larger amount. After we pay off the mortgage, we'll want to provide for the future of the kids, in addition to taking care of God's portion, just as we talked about."

"But?"

"But since this check is so much larger than we anticipated, I think you and I need to pray together and talk about what we want to tell Juan, even before we sit down with him."

"I'm glad." She nodded. "There's something else, too."

"The bank?"

She nodded. "We know each other so well! We can't deposit it here, at least not all of it."

"Agreed. I haven't taken a day off except Sunday mornings for over a month. How about next Friday, after school's out, we take the kids to our parents' place and then pick them up again Sunday evening. That will give us most of two days to relax and pray things through."

Maria was nodding as Effie walked up with a tray full of their food. "This smells wonderful! I'm starved! Effie, do you have any preserves for our toast?

"You don't like those little tubs of strawberry jelly, do you? I don't blame you! We've got some Knott's Berry Farm Boysenberry Preserves. Would you like that better?"

"Definitely!" Tom and Maria said together.

As Effie walked away to get the preserves, Maria reached across and took Tom's hands. She closed her eyes as Tom prayed, "Guide us and be glorified in our lives Lord, and bless this food we pray in Jesus' name. Amen."

"Amen." She released his hands as they opened their eyes.

"He said quietly, "Since you're not on duty this morning, why don't you go and talk to Pastor Harold to see if the church has a wish list. Tell him that the state gave us some money for the land they acquired from us through eminent domain, and we want to make a donation. Don't say how much."

"I agree. Once we know how much we're giving to Towne Community Church, we'll then decide how to distribute the remainder of our tithe of that check."

"Right." He smiled. "One of the things we're going to have to pray about is how we're going to tithe the dividends and interest year by year into the future."

"Have you called Everett Beam? I didn't dream his law firm would get us this much. I am wondering how much they're going to bill us."

"When I get back to the station, "I'll call him and thank him. I'll also ask him for suggestions with regard to our wills, now that all that this has happened."

As they were finishing their meal, Effie approached. "I forgot to ask you if you wanted some juice."

Walter nodded. "How about it, dear? I'd like some grapefruit juice. How about you?"

"I'll have orange juice."

"Okay. I'll be right back." Effie walked away, and soon she returned with the juice. "Will there be anything else?" They shook their heads. "Okay, I'll put it on your tab, Chief, okay?"

"Okay, Effie, add your twenty percent."

Effie grinned. "Thanks, Chief!"

2.

Tom put down the phone and looked up at the clock. He called out, "Jack? Go home and get some dinner. You're on patrol tonight."

Jack came to the doorway. "After Debbie and I get some dinner I'll be at home with my cell phone and radio turned on. Unless I get a call from the answering service, I won't start patrolling until 8:30 or so, okay?"

"Okay. I'll have my scanner turned on. If you get a call, and you're not on site within five minutes I'll have your butt."

He grinned. "Right, Chief."

"Good. Go home and get some dinner. I'll lock up in a few minutes."

"Okay. Good night, Chief."

"G'night."

Tom leaned back in his chair, thinking. *Dinner won't be ready until*....The phone rang, and he picked up the receiver. "Towne Police Department."

"Tom? This is Bill. I've got trouble brewing here again. Your deputy is on his way, but you said to call you."

"Okay, Bill, I'll be right there."

Tom punched another line and another number. A few seconds later, he heard Maria's voice. "Hello?"

"Hi. It's me. I'll try to be there by six, but I may be a few minutes late. I'm headed out to check on some trouble at Bill's Bar and Grill."

"Okay. I love you. Bye."

"I love you too. Bye." Hanging up, Tom moved rapidly out the door and locked up. In his patrol car, he used the siren.

It took him less than two minutes to get there. In the parking lot, Jack's patrol car's lights were flashing, but he was inside. Tom went in, and there was a quiet crowd in one corner. Jack, who was almost as big as Tom, was talking quietly to a man in a green shirt. Bill, the owner, saw Tom come in and beckoned him to the bar. Bill was shaking his head and talked quietly. "Thanks for coming, Chief. There are no broken bones, but that knucklehead in the green shirt is real trouble."

Tom walked over to the crowd in the corner. "How many of you work for J & J construction?" A half-dozen hands went up. "I'm Chief Kuster of the Towne police department. Who's your site supervisor?" There was silence. "I'll ask once again, who's your site supervisor?" Again, there was silence. "If I don't get a truthful answer you're all spending the night in jail, and we'll sort it out in front of a judge. What will it be?"

A voice in back said, "John Simpson is our supervisor."

Tom nodded. "Thank you. Tell John Simpson, I don't want any further trouble with J & J. He and I need to talk about this. I will be on-site at his double-wide trailer tomorrow morning at 6:00 AM. Can at least one of you tell him that tonight?"

There were murmurs. The same voice said, "He'll be told, but he won't like it."

Tom looked at the man in the green shirt that had made all the trouble. "You can be sure that I don't like this either, and it's best if we're on the same side. Got it?"

The man nodded.

Tom turned to Bill. "Do you want to press any charges tonight?"

Bill shook his head. "Not tonight."

"Okay. Come on, Jack. If you have to come back here tonight, just call the Highway Patrol for help, and put ALL of them in the slammer." He paused. "If they can behave themselves, they can stay to have fun, right Bill?"

"Right." Bill nodded.

Jack was moving. "I hope I don't have to come back tonight, Chief."

"So do I, Jack, so do I."

They walked out.

+ + +

As he came in the front door from the mud room, Tom was greeted with a chorus of "Hi, Dad!"

Maria gave him a hug and looked up at his face. "Dinner's almost ready. Is everything okay at Bill's?"

He nodded. "For now, I guess. I'll be leaving early in the morning again. ... I'm hungry!" He headed towards the bathroom.

After washing off some of the day's grime and sweat, he joined the family at the table. "Tommie, it's your turn to say grace, isn't it?"

The boy nodded, and they bowed their heads. "Father, please bless this food and bless us. In Jesus' name. Amen." They all began to eat in silence. Then Tommie spoke again. "Dad, did you know that there's a cave on the hill east of the swimming hole?"

Tom paused from eating. "On the west side of the hill east of the swimming hole?"

"Yes."

"No I didn't." He swallowed. "It must have opened after that little quake we had last week. How big is it?"

"I had to stoop to go in, but my flashlight wouldn't shine far enough to see the back of the cave. You have to be near the opening to see it because of the boulders."

"That's interesting!"

"Yeah. I didn't think you'd wanted anyone else going in there until you had checked it out, so I covered the opening with some leafy branches."

"That's great, Tommie. What time do you get home from school tomorrow?"

"There's no soccer practice, so I should be back here by 3:30."

"All right. Tommie, you and I will check it out tomorrow. I don't want the rest of you to come along until after Tommie and I check it out, okay?"

Alice said, "Why can't I go? I'm eleven, and I'll be twelve in two months."

Tom smiled. "Yes you are, Alice, but I don't know what dangers might be in the cave yet, so let's wait on that, okay?"

"Okay."

"Dad, will I get to see it?" asked Karen. "I just turned eight."

Maria laughed. "Karen, my sweet, you and I will get to see it when we're sure everything is safe, won't we Dad?" She looked at him.

Tom nodded. "Karen, did you have your piano lesson today?"

"Yeah, Dad, she said I did great!"

"Excellent."

They continued to eat, and there was constant chatter around the table, even after dessert."

+ + +

The next morning, Tom went straight to the J & J construction site trailer. Standing in front of the door was a muscular man of medium height. "Good morning. You must be Chief Kuster."

Tom offered his hand, and as they shook he said, "Yes, I'm Chief Tom Kuster. Are you John Simpson?"

"Yeah. Come on inside. It's warmer." They went up the steps and into the trailer. "One of my men gave me his version of what happened. What can you tell me?" He gestured to a chair, and he sat down when Tom did.

Tom was serious. "The night before last, it was just a matter of a waitress getting squeezed inappropriately and your man getting decked by her. She's well trained in the martial arts by one of my deputies. The guy didn't like it, and some of your other men had to restrain him."

John Simpson grinned. "He was rubbing his jaw off and on all day. What happened last night?"

"By the time I arrived, Jack, my deputy was already there, and things had simmered down. I talked to the owner, and he likes the business your crew brings him, but he doesn't put up with violent trouble. He did not press any charges last night, but if there is trouble again, I'm sure he will."

"What would happen then?"

"It depends upon what charges are leveled. Thus far, the local reporter for *The Register* has not paid any attention, or at least has not put anything in the paper. She hangs around the county courthouse downtown, and she's really good at what she does. Her name is Barbara. If charges are brought, you can be certain she'll get it to the front page. You don't want that to happen, and you can be sure that I don't either."

"Meaning?"

"Towne is generally quiet and peaceful. A front-page story about J & J will bring in television crews, and I don't want them under foot. Do you?

John Simpson scowled. "No."

Tom shrugged. "As far as I'm concerned, this is all in the past, now. Your men are your business, and I'm not concerned unless I have to make an arrest. I'm not your enemy, and I'm not giving you any ultimatums. I'm simply here to tell you how things are in this area. There's just me and my three deputies, but we all do our jobs and do them well. I've had my say with you this morning. What you do from here on in is up to you. Am I being clear enough?

For the first time that morning, John Simpson smiled. "Yes, you're very clear. You're being more than fair with at least one of my men, and I appreciate it. Do you want me to fire him?"

Tom shook his head. "That's up to you. If he was just letting off a little steam, and it is not a pattern, I'm good with whatever action you may choose – or not choose – to take." He got up. "Thanks for meeting me." He shook John's hand again. "Have a good day."

"You too."

They both went back outside, and soon Tom's patrol car was raising dust as he left the site. John scratched his head, put on a helmet, and went to work.

At a signal on the edge Towne, Tom pushed a button on his dash. "Jenelle, are you in yet?"

"This is Charly. Jenelle's coming in later, remember? What's up Chief?

"I just talked to John Simpson at the construction site about what's been happening at Bill's. I hope that's the end of it. I'm headed to the station and then on out to the high school to see Mike Robbins. He usually starts early like I do."

"Roger that."

Tom put the mike in the clip, and he drove downtown. About a block from the station, he parked his patrol car on a side street facing Main. Getting out of the car, he started toward the station. Suddenly, he stopped. He heard a subtle sound like a whimper coming from the shadow of an alley between two buildings. On a hunch, he turned in that direction. As he got closer, he noticed a woman trying to draw deeper into the shadow, crouching behind a trash dumpster. "Anna? Is that you?"

"I'm okay, Chief. Please don't come closer."

"What's wrong Anna?"

"Please! I don't want any trouble!"

"This is not about trouble. Why are you crying?"

There was a pause. "Please go away."

As he got closer, Tom could see that she had been badly beaten up. He stopped. "Stay right there. I'll pull my car into the alley. Don't move, okay?"

"Please! I'll be okay. Just leave me alone."

"I can't, Anna. Just stay right where you are. I'll bring the car to you. Okay?"

There was silence. Then softly she responded. "Okay, Chief."

Walking purposely and rapidly, Tom went back to the patrol car and got in. As soon as the engine came to life, he pulled into the alley and unlocked the back door. Anna got in. "You're safe now, Anna. Leave everything to me." He reached for his mike. "Charly, this is Tom."

"Yeah, Chief, this is Charly."

"Do you remember Jenelle's uncle on her Mom's side moving here last month?"

"Yeah, I remember."

"Right. Call Jenelle. Have her call him and tell him I need a favor in the form of some confidential and legal first aid, because I don't want to use the hospital. Tell Jenelle to call me only if its not okay. I know where he lives, and I'll be there in about six or seven minutes if its okay. Got it?"

"Roger and out."

Tom put the mike back in the clip. "Anna, Maria and I met this doctor about two weeks ago. You'll like him. He'll fix you up and make you feel better. Then I'll take you somewhere safe."

"Please don't take me home."

"No, Anna, that's not what I have in mind. Just trust me, okay?"

"I trust you Chief."

"Good. Would you like to talk about it before we get to the doctor?"

She hesitated. "When Toby and I got married, he wasn't like this. He didn't start losing his temper until after I miscarried."

"When was that?"

"A little over a year ago. We tried counseling, but it didn't help. I love him, but I can't take this. I think I have to divorce him." She sat back and relaxed against the seat as Tom drove silently.

Tom slowed down. "Here we are." Tom pulled into a driveway, turned off the engine, and got out. He gave Debbie a hand as she slowly and painfully got out of the patrol car. "You don't need to say anything, but I'm getting you into a shelter, and then we'll help you get a lawyer. Okay?"

"Okay."

A white-haired gentleman came down the porch steps to meet them. "Hello there, I'm Dr. Johnson. Come this way." He led her up the steps.

3.

After Tom saw that Anna felt comfortable in the shelter, he told the director to call him if there was a problem with getting her a good lawyer. It was late in the morning when he headed back to Towne and its high school. A few flakes of early snow were falling. As he drove up, he saw Mike Robbins standing beside his car. Tom rolled down his window. "Good morning! Any problems with the fire safety inspection?"

The Fire Chief shook his head. "No. A couple of the kids who gave me static last year seem to have grown up some. Gary Pope is currently dating Jim Hickman's daughter, Jody, and she's smart enough not to put up with any nonsense from him. The other one's Dennis Statton, and he fancies himself to be a songwriter at the moment, and I'm no longer on his radar."

Tom smiled. "Good. Gary and Jody are both smart kids. I think they'll probably go to Sacramento State together. Dennis might get into Cal-State Long Beach's "Promising Composers" program if he can get his act together." He paused. "Do you need me for anything?"

"Not really, but your son Tommie took me aside and told me about his discovery. Would you mind if I tag along with the two of you?"

"Not at all! Why not?"

"I've got a portable flood light at the fire station with a backpack power supply and other flashlights. If the cave is large, the floodlight might be handy to have."

"Good – bring it along. I'll meet you and Tommie at my house this afternoon at about 3:30."

"Okay, see you then." Mike got into his car as Tom drove off.

For a little over two hours, Tom drove Towne's streets, patrolling. In a larger community, such duty would be left to the deputies, but Towne was small, and Tom did a little of everything.

After getting some lunch, Tom drove out to the railroad tracks on the northwest side of town. The railroad had put in new crossing bars to go with the flashing lights. He parked nearby until a train came, so he could see that the crossing guard equipment was working correctly. Tom had made hundreds of phone calls over a period of four years to get the safety bars installed.

In the middle of the afternoon, he headed back towards Towne. Tom parked the patrol car in front of his house. Going to the garage, he backed out his four-wheel-drive pickup truck. Inside the garage, he picked up a rechargeable spotlight and a couple of smaller flashlights, along with some safety glasses. Putting it all in the cab behind the seat, he closed the truck's door and headed to the back porch of his house.

As he went inside into the mud room, Maria was standing in the doorway to the kitchen. "Hi, handsome."

He kissed her. "Hi, beautiful. Is Tommie ready to go?"

"No, I told him he'd have to go back to the cave another time. Tommie's come down with a bad cold, and I don't want him going out again. If his throat gets worse, I'll keep him home from school tomorrow."

"Tomorrow is Friday. If he goes to school, we can pack everybody up in the afternoon and go to San Francisco like we talked about. If he doesn't go to school, then we'll just delay our San Francisco trip for a week. How does that sound?"

"Let's delay it for a week anyway. Our trip to San Francisco can wait. If he's traveling with us with a bad cold, it not only might get passed to the rest of us, but your parents might catch it."

"Okay. Call the folks and tell them we won't come until next weekend." He paused and nodded. "Mike will be here in a few minutes. He's going spelunking with me."

"Spelunking?" Maria raised her eyebrows.

"Yeah. Many people call it caving. Speleology is the study of caves and their environments. This might be just an abandoned gold mine that has surfaced after all these years. Mike and I will check it out." There was a knock at the door behind them. "Come in, Mike!"

Smiling, Mike said, "Hi, Maria." He looked at Tom. "I saw you putting things in your truck as I was driving up, so I put my stuff in there rather than take both trucks."

Maria smiled. "It sounds like you men are going to have fun. Tom, I can delay dinner a half-hour or so, to give you some more time. Tommie's not very hungry anyway."

Tom nodded. "Good idea."

Mike raised his eyebrows. "Tommie's not hungry? Is this world of ours coming to an end?" He grinned. "What's the story?"

She smiled. "He's got a bad cold and the start of a sore throat. He's not going with you."

Tom nodded. "Right." He kissed Maria on the cheek. "See you later. ... Let's go, Mike."

The two men silently went out to the truck, and soon they were driving down a dirt road into the hills behind Tom's house. After about three-quarters of a mile, they saw the small lake everyone called the swimming hole. Tom veered off to the east side and parked on the side of the hill about a hundred yards from the lake.

Mike began putting on a small backpack containing batteries for his floodlight. "Unofficial rules of caving say we should each carry three flashlights."

"Right," Tom nodded, "Do you want one of these pairs of safety glasses?"

"Thanks. I brought along a couple of respirators, but I hope we won't need them. I'll leave them here in the truck. Where are we going?" Mike looked up the hill.

Tom pointed. "Based upon Tommie's description, I'd guess it's in the area of those boulders. I think we'd better put on our gloves."

"Agreed," said Mike. Doing so, they started hiking upward. The hill was very steep, and when they reached a point just below the boulders, they stopped to get their breath. Mike grinned. "I'm suddenly feeling older, when I remember how Tommie described this. You would have thought that he had made little more effort than crossing the street!"

They chuckled. Tom pointed, "You go towards that side, and I'll go up this side." They split up, and the hill was even steeper. Mike spotted a pile of branches leaning between two of the boulders. "I think I've found it."

"I agree."

Mike looked up, and Tom was standing on one of the boulders, above him, but Tom rapidly climbed down and stood next to his friend. They both quickly pulled away the branches that covered an opening about five feet tall and four feet wide. Mike turned on his floodlight, and as it hummed softly, he stooped over and went in.

Tom was right behind him. "That flood of yours puts out a lot of light!"

"Yeah, I've got a special lens on this thing, and I could light up the grandstand at the football field with it." After walking about a dozen steps, Mike stood up.

Sweeping the flood from side to side, he whistled. "Man!"

Tom stood up next to him, saying, "Wow! This cave must be at least fifty yards wide and, what do you think, thirty yards from here to that opening over there?"

Mike nodded. "That's about right, I think." He swung the flood from side to side. "I don't think we're the first ones who were ever here, do you?"

Tom's voice was quieter. "No." He turned on his spotlight and swung it upward. "I'm surprised how dry it is in here. That peak height must be more than fifty feet. I don't see any dripping from the walls or ceiling."

He shook his head. "Neither do I. You follow the perimeter to the right and I'll go left. I'll meet you at the opening over there on the far side."

As Mike moved to the left, Tom began to examine the right-hand side in detail with his spotlight. He noticed that he was climbing slightly. "Hey, Mike, "I think this side is a little higher. There's a raised area over here. I'm going to check it out." Tom began to climb.

Mike called back, "Okay."

There was a pause. "Okay, I'm coming down again. I took a few pictures."

"You took pictures? I didn't know you had a camera."

"This is my work jacket, and I carry a sensitive but small point-and-shoot. It has good resolution, its waterproof, and its got a nice zoom."

"Cool."

In about five minutes, they reached the opening on the far side of the cave. Tom pointed his spotlight at the walls either side of the opening. "This is not rock. It's some kind of bricks!"

"So it seems! Let's go inside." They went in.

Tom said in a stage whisper, "Good Lord!"

"What?"

"This is some kind of chapel. Do you see the cross on that wall, with the altar below it?" He pointed his spotlight off to the right.

Mike swung the floodlight around. Softly, he said, "I see it. There's some stuff on that low shelf over there." Tom took some pictures. Mike walked over, and he reached to touch what he saw.

"Hold it!" Tom was intense. "If all of this is as old as I think it is, it's very fragile, so don't touch it this time."

"Thanks, you're right." Mike looked at his watch. "Not knowing the air quality, let's start making our way out."

"Okay."

A beeping tone came from Mike's belt. He uncliped a meter and looked at it under the diffused light of the flood. "There's some kind of flammable gas in here. It's not at a dangerous level." He took a small bottle out of his jacket pocket. "I'll take an air sample and take it to the lab my department has on call." He unscrewed the lid from the bottle, waved it in the air, and screwed the lid back on. He put it in his pocket again.

Tom started to move, but he stopped. Moving slightly to his right, he went to a low platform. "This looks like...." He reached out and lifted a heavy cloth. "Shine your flood over here, Mike."

"Is that a skull?"

"Yep." Tom took a picture and then put the blanket in place again. "Let's get out of here, go back to the truck, and talk about strategy."

Silently, they walked rapidly back to the entrance of the cave, stooped down, and made their way out. Outside, daylight was waning, and Tom took a picture of the cave entrance. As they walked away and down,

Tom took pictures of the area. Snow was falling steadily. When they got to the truck, they got in, and they silently sat there for several minutes.

Mike was the first to speak. "So, do you have a strategy in mind?"

"Yeah. I've got a couple of two-by-fours here in back, and I've got an 8x10 canvas tarp and a couple of quarts of 'Rex-Hex' glue. It will stick to just about anything, wet or dry. We're both wearing our work jackets. Have you got some danger stickers in one of your bigger pockets?"

"Always! I'm beginning to see your strategy. What stickers do you have in mind?"

Nodding, Tom said, "I'd like a 'Danger' with a skull and crossbones if you got one, and a 'Poisonous Gas' sticker. I've got yellow 'Police Line Do Not Cross' tape."

Mike grinned. "I'm with you! Let's get started."

It took about ten minutes. They glued two-by-fours parallel to the long edges of the tarp, about a foot from the edges. Then after wedging one two by four into the rocks close to the ground, they stretched the tarp upward and fastened the top in the same way. All around the perimeter they inserted glue between the rocks and the tarp wherever they could. Mike stuck two 'danger' stickers near to the center of their work, and next he stuck 'poisonous gas' stickers in several places. Tom stretched a police tape across the whole thing.

They stepped back to look at their work. Tom nodded. "That looks pretty secure. We may have to redo things in the spring."

"I agree. What are we going to say about what we found?"

Tom was serious. "Mike, this is on my property, and I'd like to keep things simple, not saying much.

First of all, aren't all flammable gases at least potentially poisonous?"

"Absolutely!"

"Then let's be purposely vague with everyone. We found a moderate-sized cave, but it had some poisonous gas, so the opening has been legally sealed by the Chief of Police and the Fire Chief. How's that sound?"

Mike laughed. "I like it! It's not a lie, but we're not telling all that we know."

"Right!"

As Tom started the engine, Mike was now more serious. "Just between us, what do you think so far of what we found?"

"I'll print out the pictures for a file I'll keep locked up at the station. Let's get together next Monday morning, or maybe Tuesday morning, and discuss what we see in the pictures."

Mike nodded. "Yeah, but what do you think right now?"

Tom put the truck in gear and started down the hill. "We both noticed the torch sockets in both areas. We've only just begun to explore, and I'm looking forward to seeing more next Spring, even if we have to wear respirators. My best initial guess is that this cave is an undocumented mission of Junipero Serra or one of his contemporaries. That would date what we saw from somewhere in the late eighteenth century to the early nineteenth century."

"This is amazing!" Mike was smiling. "Do you say this because of the altar and cross? I think what I almost touched was a Bible, a journal, or both."

Tom slowed down a little. "You're probably right about that, but the books aren't what convinced me."

"What then?"

"It was the skeleton. Did you notice the cloth that seemed to partially surround the skull? That was an alb. An alb is a hooded robe worn by priests, and California's missions were all planted by the Franciscans."

"Don't you need to investigate the skeleton more?"

"I think it can wait until next spring or summer, especially with the whole cave sealed. Will your lab make the test results of that air sample available to the public?"

Mike was thoughtful. "I think if I have it tested at my own personal expense, the report won't even be part of official records."

Tom nodded. "I'll reimburse you for the expense. I can afford it. Meanwhile, I'm not even going to tell Tommie or Maria about what we found in the cave except the flammable gas. I think that's the best way for me. How about you?"

"I'll do the same. I won't even tell Jenelle, though that will be hard. Besides, it's your property, and that makes it all your decisions. I hope that we can tell our spouses next Spring after we know more."

"I'm not sure we can keep it totally secret even that long." Tom stopped his truck next to his garage. He looked at his watch. "We timed this pretty well. Tell Jenelle I'll see her tomorrow morning."

"Okay. This has been a real adventure." Mike smiled. "Thanks for letting me tag along. I think that the adventure is just beginning though." He opened the door. "See ya!"

"See ya!" As Mike got into his truck and drove off, Tom walked toward the back porch and went in. Aromas from the kitchen greeted his nose.

4.

A week later, Tom and his family loaded up Maria's minivan, and they drove to San Francisco. Mike and Trina Kuster were delighted to have their grandchildren for the weekend. After greetings and hugs, Tom and Maria headed north to Golden Gate Park.

There was scattered sunshine on the water, but the wind was blowing, and it was cold. Finding shelter from the wind in a gazebo, they sat down and huddled together. Maria was thoughtful. "I like it here. It's beautiful."

"Hmmm. Yes," mumbled Tom.

"Losing a few apple trees to the highway expansion has had me thinking about the wasted fruit."

"Wasted? You make a lot of applesauce every year and give it away."

"True, and we also let the high school pick apples and sell them to raise money for things they want, but there are still apples unpicked. Animals get some of them, but a couple of weeks ago I found bushels of apples lying on the ground."

Tom looked at her. "Really! I haven't explored the hills behind the house much in the last few years, so I hadn't noticed."

Maria nodded. "I know. Being Chief of Police is time-consuming for you. What about the shelter you took Anna to a week ago? How is it doing?"

"Oh, it gets by, I guess. There are times when they have to ask for help with food. Being a non-profit they have their struggles and depend on donations."

She smiled. "They have a large kitchen. I wonder if they would be interested in canning and selling applesauce?"

Tom shook his head. "They might, but the staff is kept pretty busy, and those being sheltered couldn't pick the apples, let alone transport them."

"Maybe not, but volunteers could do the picking, and take the apples to the fire station. Then getting the apples to the shelter would be easy."

Tom smiled. "That sounds great! Do you want to organize it over the summer if the shelter goes for it?"

Maria nodded. "Sure! I have the time, but...."

"But what?"

"Are we avoiding talking about investments?"

Tom nodded. "I guess we are. Where do you want to begin?"

She smiled. "I already have. Last week, when we were having those three days of early snow, I spent a lot of time looking out my office window at the snow and praying." She paused. "I think we should set aside enough for the kids' college or trade school educations, and have the rest set up to give us steady income and growth. Juan can advise us on that."

"Right. I have made an appointment with him for breakfast tomorrow morning at our hotel."

Tom looked at her. "I can feel you shivering. Why don't we go to the hotel? We can pray and meditate almost as easily there as here, and it'll be a lot warmer."

"Good! This humid cold goes to our bones!" They stood up and walked briskly to the van. It only took them about fifteen minutes to get to the hotel and get checked in.

+ + +

Saturday breakfast the next morning was interesting and fun. Juan Smith was a wiry Hispanic in his thirties, and he had a dry sense of humor. He worked in an independent brokerage office that specialized in socially responsible investments.

After cracking more than a few jokes about the investments and investors, Juan spoke quietly as he got down to business. "I have been curious why you wanted to meet in person. I know you got some money from the state, and we talked on the phone about investing for your kid's education. Has something changed?"

Tom reached into a pocket, and he gave Juan a photocopy of the check. Juan's eyes got wider. "Carrumba!"

Tom smiled. "Amen! We still want to set up education IRAs for the kids, but we also want to talk about growth and income for the future."

Maria nodded. "We want all of it to be in socially responsible investments."

"Good." Reaching into his briefcase, Juan handed Maria a folder. "In here is information on some of the best in the socially responsible sector of the market. In addition, there are mutual fund companies," he pointed to some names, "that can provide you with a money market checking account tied to your portfolio."

Maria was thoughtful. "Good. We want to start by donating twenty percent off the top, divided among these church charities." She handed Juan a list. "Then we want you to cut a check for ten percent of the gross to us that we can deposit in our own All American Bank in Towne."

Tom nodded. "I took one of your business reply mail envelopes, endorsed the check 'for deposit only,' and mailed it to you with a deposit slip for our account with your firm yesterday. You'll probably get it in Monday's mail."

Juan nodded. "Okay. I'll cut these checks for you that same day and send them to you express overnight." He paused. "Now, if you have the time, let's talk about some of these companies and mutual funds."

Their talk continued through most of the morning. After Juan left, Tom and Maria changed clothes, and spent their time at the hotel's indoor pool and other recreation facilities.

+ + +

Sunday morning was a new kind of experience for all of them – Tom, Maria, Tom's Parents, and the kids. Maria had heard that a church not far from downtown San Francisco had grown to one of the largest in the country in a short time. Community Evangelical Church looked like it seated over 5000. The worship area had two large high-definition video screens, along with a sound system that the kids loved. In the front they counted more than ten instrumentalists, many of whom sang, and another twenty that also sang.

The six or seven songs at the beginning included rock, country, and more traditional selections. As Tom glanced down their row, his family and everyone around them seemed almost electrified with joy. It was energizing for all of them, including his parents. The congregation that day included many ethnic groups, and most people were casually dressed, though a few wore suits and dresses.

After worship, the kids were invited to church school, so after the adults saw where the kids would be for the next hour, they went to a lower area where there were a variety of snacks and beverages. While Maria and Trina chatted animatedly with several other women, Tom and his Dad gradually moved towards a large group of men. In an area with hundreds of books arranged neatly on shelves, the men were talking about the mission days.

A tall and thin man with white hair and beard had everyone's attention. "Mission San Francisco de Asisi, was founded in June of 1776. It was the sixth mission of Francisco Palóu and Junípero Serra. It's also known as Mission Delores, and it is the oldest surviving building in San Francisco."

"Isn't it a historical landmark?"

"Yes, but with budget cuts, the state has not been keeping it up as well as it should. Our church is helping the Catholic Archdiocese with some much-needed repairs. That's why we took a special offering this morning."

Tom cleared his throat. "Are all the original missions well-documented?"

The man nodded. "As far as we know, there were twenty-one military and religious outposts that were established by Catholic priests to educate and defend Native Americans and expand Christianity. At one time, there were rumors of other outposts, but two hundred years have passed, so they're probably all documented."

Mike quietly turned to his son. "Why did you ask that?"

Tom smiled. He murmured, "I'll tell you all about it in a few months."

"I have to wait, heh?"

Tom nodded. "Yep."

The white-haired man was continuing. "As many of you know, our church has acquired a small building in the mission district. It's going to be turned into an ecumenical museum of California Church History. We already have some nice items for display. If we can acquire enough things more for our collection, we hope to open it to the public later this year." He looked at his watch. "I've got to go. I've got grand kids getting out of church school in five minutes."

Mike turned to his son and said, "Let's get our wives and go get the kids."

Tom nodded. "Right." They started walking towards the women." If you and Mom want to join us, Maria and I are taking the kids to the zoo for lunch. You can meet us there in your own car, and then all of us can go straight home afterward. I want to have the kids in bed by 9:00."

"I'll check with Trina, but I think we'd both enjoy going to the zoo. We haven't been there for over three months. I'm on the Board of Directors now."

The four of them walked over to the education wing of the church, and when the kids saw them, they ran up, and all of them talked excitedly about their experiences. The kids continued to chatter as they transferred their suitcases from their grandparents' car to the van. Then, the excitement continued as they drove to the zoo.

The zoo was originally named Fleishhacker Zoo, named for its founder, Herbert Felishhacker, who was a banker and Parks Commission President. They began construction in 1929 next to what was then the country's largest swimming pool. The zoo covers more than one hundred acres.

That day, Tommie stayed close to his Dad and his grandpa, while Maria and Trina kept control of the girls. After having hamburgers, mountains of French fries, and gallons of pop, they began exploring the zoo.

While they were listening to a zookeeper talk about the big cats, Mike leaned over and whispered, "I don't suppose your secret has something to do with that cave that Tommie discovered?"

"The cave is polluted with methane. I've got a police-enforced safety barricade in place because methane is both poisonous and flammable."

"Oh." Mike paused. "Can you give me another hint?"

Tom hesitated. "Do you remember how many stacks of old books were damaged when our roof leaked when I was fifteen? We boxed them up and mostly forgot them in the basement."

"Yeah."

"I've been interested in old books ever since, no matter how old, damaged, or dusty. That's all I'll say right now."

"Okay." Mike looked at his son with a sly grin. He knew his son very well, and noticed what Tom had not said. He turned his attention back to the zookeeper and his lecture on the big cats. Maria and Trina talked in low whispers. The kids didn't notice anything the adults were talking about.

When the talk on the big cats was over, the kids wanted to hear about the raptors, so they stayed for that as well. When they stood up at the end, Mike stretched, and then he said, "I think Trina and I have had enough for one day. The rest of you might want to stay longer, but I think we'll head home."

Trina nodded. "Amen to that!"

As they were walking towards the main gate, Tommie asked, can we stay longer, Dad? Mom?"

Maria looked at Tom with a very subtle shake of her head. Tom responded, "Not today, Tommie. We've got a long drive ahead before we get home, and we'll have to stop for dinner on the way.

The kids all said, "Ohhhh."

Tom smiled. "Where shall we stop for dinner? Do you want to go to that big pizza place in the valley that has the game room?"

"Yeah!" the kids cheered, and the adults laughed.

Trina pointed, "Our car's this way, and you're going that way. Let's say our good-byes here."

Everyone hugged, and Mike and Trina gave their grand kids kisses. Then they went their separate

ways. The Pizza stop was a lot longer than either
Maria or Tom had planned. By the time they got the
kids bathed and into bed, and by the time they had
showered and had their pillow talk, it was well after
midnight. During the night, Tom vaguely heard chatter
on his scanner, but he slept soundly until his alarm
went off at 5:30.

5.

As Tom walked into the station Monday morning, Jenelle said, "6:30? You must have tied one on!"

He grinned. "Hardly. We were in San Francisco for the weekend and got home late."

"Did you hear anything on your scanner last night?"

Tom stopped in his doorway. "No. Did anything happen?"

"Charly and Jack covered it. Charly filled me in just before he left on patrol about ten minutes ago. That troublemaker named…" she paused as she looked down at her desk, "named Bob Charger from J & J Construction died accidentally. I think last night's report is on your desk."

Tom shook his head. "Thanks, I'll look at it. What a way to begin a Monday!" He went to the table in the corner, made himself a cup of Earl Grey, and sat down at his desk.

He read it through, then he went back and read it more slowly. After taking a swallow of tea, Tom leaned back in his chair. After a moment, he leaned forward again. "Jenelle? You talked to Charly. What do you think?"

She came to his doorway. "Considering his previous violence, this seems almost anticlimactic. He somehow found out where Judy lives, went up on her porch and knocked. When she came to her door, he tried to barge in. She was trained for it. After she crushed his groin, he's bent over and staggering backward. He fell, and when he landed he broke his neck. Probably died instantly. Judy called 911. Charly was there less than three minutes later because he had been getting a cup of coffee at the Hen. Charly checked for a carotid pulse. Dead. That's it." The phone rang. "I'll get it." Jenelle went back to her desk and picked up her phone.

Tom picked up the report and read it again. He could hear Jenelle's voice but not her words.

She came back to his door. "That was the Coroner. Bob Charger's blood-alcohol level was way up there. The Coroner said he found a scuff mark at the top of Judy's stairs that confirms Judy's story. He's calling it accidental." The phone rang again. Back at her desk Jenelle picks up the receiver and only listens for a moment. She calls out, "Chief! It's for you! It's Mike."

"Thanks." He picked up line one. "Hey, Mike, what's up?"

"Tom, I got the report on that bottle sample. It had about one-hundredth of one-percent methane. The concentration would have to be about five percent to explode."

"Good. It's safe. How much do those meters cost?"

Mike paused. "If you're gonna buy one it'll cost you about $175 for a decent one."

Tom was thoughtful. "I think I'm going to get one and keep it handy."

"That may be a good idea. I'll give you the lab receipt when I see ya."

"Okay. We've both got work to do. See ya later."

"Yeah, later."

Tom was thoughtful, taking a swallow of tea. He picked up the phone again, looked in his rotary card index, and punched a number. "Hello, this is Chief Tom Kuster. May I speak with Ruth Branch please?" He paused.

The rather husky voice of the librarian answered. "Chief Kuster, what can I do for you?"

"Yes, hi Ruth. ... I've got a question. Someone told me that you have a hobby of finding, identifying, and sometimes selling rare books. Is that right?

"Yes! Why do you ask?"

"I was talking with my Dad over the weekend, and I mentioned to him some books we have in the basement of the house. I haven't seen them since I was a teenager because hardly anyone ever goes down there. Some of the books seemed very old when I was in high school. I keep the basement locked. If you're interested in seeing if any of them are worth anything, tell Maria. This winter, when there's snow on the ground and things slow down, the two of you can do some exploring. What do you think?" A chill went up Tom's spine, but he didn't know why.

"That sounds interesting. I'll talk to Maria. Maybe after the holidays in January we can check your basement out."

The other line started ringing, but Jenelle picked it up. Tom continued, "That sounds good, Ruth. I..."

Jenelle called out, "Code 3! Train derailed! Northwest spur!"

Tom said, "Ruth I've got to go! Emergency! Bye!" He slammed down the phone, pulled his coat off the rack and moved fast. He and Jenelle reached the door at the same time. Tom said, "Let's take just my car."

"Right! I think I hear one of the fire horns. Mike's probably on his way there too." In the patrol car, they belted up.

With lights and siren, they sped off. He kept it under fifty until he reached the edge of town, then he floored it. Tom had taken the California Highway Patrol's high speed driving course, and he used all of those skills.

Jenelle pointed, "I see flames, but those are at least five miles away!" Suddenly, flames shot into the sky, and a moment later they felt the thud of the explosion hit the car. "Wow! That was some explosion! I hope no one was killed."

"Yeah." Tom focused on his driving. As they approached, there were several smaller explosions. A tear rolled down Tom's cheek.

Before getting out of the car, Jenelle glanced at Tom and saw the tear. "What's wrong, Tom?"

"Jenelle, ... I think this is going to be really bad for both of us." As he got out, he zipped up his jacket, because despite the heat of the fire in front of them, a cold wind was at their backs. Tom walked up to a fireman standing by a hydrant, and nodded to him.

"Hey Chief. Hey Jenelle."

"Hey Brad. She smiled. "What's the latest?"

"The train derailed about twenty yards northeast of the road. It plowed through a van waiting at the crossing and kept going into those storage buildings."

They both nodded. Jenelle asked, "Do you know what caused that big explosion?"

"Yeah. When everything finally stopped, the van was engulfed in flames. Mike and Bob started running over to do what they could. Just as they got to the car and started using CO_2, a tank car about twenty feet away exploded. All of us were knocked to the ground. I never imagined an explosion could be that hot!"

Tom pointed. "The explosion was over there?"

"Yeah, where that crater is."

"What was in the tanker car?"

"Hydrogen. That fire's all out except for a few small spots."

Tom started running towards the crater, and Jenelle ran after him. Just before they got to the crater, they stopped. Tom started shaking, and he sat down on the ground. He was shaking and sobbing.

Jenelle looked. "Oh, Tom...."

Sobbing, Tom said, "Maria and the kids were going shopping at the mall...."

Tears were running down Jenelle's cheeks. Oh, Tom...."

Tom stopped crying for a moment. "Jenelle, look at me." She looked at his face. "Jenelle, we might not find Mike or Bob."

"What? Why?"

"They were in the explosion. Hydrogen burns at more than twice the temperature of an acetylene torch."

"Dear Jesus!" She began to sob. They held each other until some emergency technicians wanted to take them to the hospital. Jenelle shook her head. "We weren't here when it happened. It's his family in that van, and my husband...." She choked.... "was in the explosion. We're going back to the Towne police station."

"Okay.... We're really sorry, truly sorry." The emergency technicians walked off.

"Come on, Tom, let's go back to the station. We're not needed here."

"Yeah." They got up. Slowly, they walked to the patrol car, in a daze. Some people called out their condolences to them, and they just waved, got into the car, and drove off.

"Jenelle, do you want to work, or do you want to go home?"

"Thanks for asking, but I'd rather be working than sitting at home and thinking about Mike."

"The same here." He handed her the mike. "Tell Charly and Jack they're getting overtime for the next week or so. No, wait. Give me the mike." She handed it to him. He pressed the button. "Dispatch, this is Chief Kuster."

"Hello Chief. I just heard. We're so sorry. Give Jenelle our best too."

"Thanks, she's right here and heard you. Does Bob Constantine know what's happened?"

"Yes, Chief, he was briefed a few minutes ago."

"Good. Ask him if he can loan me a few CHP deputies for a week."

"Roger, Chief."

"Over and out." Tom put the mike in the clip and looked at Jenelle. "Would you like to stop at the church with me?"

"Oh, yes, that would be good."

As they pulled up in front of the church, Pastor Harold Gentle and his wife came out the door to greet them. The pastor said, "When I saw your car turn the corner, I thought you might be dropping by... Jenelle ... Tom. You both have our condolences."

Tom nodded. "I haven't asked Jenelle, but I just want to pray for a while."

She also nodded. "Yes, I'd also like to pray for a while."

The pastor nodded. "Okay, I'll be in the church office if you need me."

Tom and Jenelle walked down toward the front of the church and stopped just short of the steps. Tom's eyes were focused on a large cross about twenty feet away, hanging above the baptistery. "Master, you suffered on your cross for about six hours. You know what happened today. It looked like no one suffered more than an instant or so. I guess I'm thankful for that." He stopped and closed his eyes. "Master, I know you're not at fault for this, but I must confess, I'm mad! Mad!" He began to shake as he did out at the crash site, and he dropped to his knees.

Jenelle had been watching, looking back and forth between Tom and the cross. When he dropped to his knees, she quietly knelt beside him. "Lord

Jesus, I don't know what to say except that I love you, and I'm glad I know you're always in my heart."

They were silent for nearly an hour except for a few sobs. Then Tom prayed, "Master. I know that Maria, Tommie, Alice, and Karen love you. It's at least some comfort to know that they're in your loving arms now and for eternity." He paused. "Mike and I talked about you several times through the years. I know that he loved you before he loved Jenelle, and he loves her passionately. So Master, I ask for both Jenelle and I, that you be patient with us, and grant both of us the healing that only you can provide in your good time. Jenelle is a fine woman, and I ask that you give her a sense of your presence whenever she feels lonely without Mike. In Jesus' name, I pray."

After about ten more minutes, Tom stood up. Jenelle looked up, and he offered her his hand. She took it as he helped her up. They walked out and were in the squad car before Jenelle spoke. "Tom, thank you for praying for me."

"I'm thankful the Lord gave me the words I needed to say."

As they pulled up to the station and got out of the car, there were two highway patrol officers waiting for them on the steps. A tall and muscular patrolman about Tom's size stepped forward. "You must be Chief Tom Kuster. I'm Cappy Coleman, and this is Charlyn Williams. I'm sorry. I don't know your name." He looked at Jenelle.

"Hi, I'm Jenelle Robbins, the wife..." her voice caught, "the widow of the Fire Chief that died in the explosion."

Charlyn Williams stepped forward. "Jenelle, can I give you a hug?"

"Sure!" They hugged, while Cappy and Tom shook hands.

Tom looked at Cappy, saying, "Are you two on loan from the CHP?"

"Sort of." Cappy was very professional "I live about fifteen miles north of here, and Charlyn lives in the same vicinity. As partners, we're in the Towne vicinity, typically patrolling just north of you. For the next couple of weeks, those of us who patrol on the north and west sides will come into town as far as the courthouse two or three times every shift."

Jenelle pointed east. "Will there be patrols south and east?"

Charlyn nodded. "Yes. Another CHP office dispatches patrols on that side of you, and they'll do something similar, coming as far as the courthouse."

Tom nodded. "Okay, thanks for dropping by. I assume that dispatch knows about all this?"

Cappy nodded. "Right." He started to move. "If you need us, we'll be in the neighborhood. It was good to meet you. You both have our condolences." He shook Tom's hand and headed for their car.

Charlyn hugged Jenelle again. "Call me if you want to talk. I'm so sorry."

"Thanks. It was good to meet you two."

A moment later, they were headed north out of town.

Tom looked at Jenelle. "I hope we're busy."

"Me too."

They went inside.

6.

On the day of the funeral and graveside services, State and nearby regional emergency services stepped in so that all those in the Towne police and fire departments could attend. It was standing room only at Towne Community Church, with the service broadcast by the local American Video System affiliate as well as the AVS cable station. Pastor Gentle's service, which lasted almost exactly an hour, was well received. There were parked cars and trucks for nearly a half mile around Towne's Community Memorial Cemetery for the graveside service. The Little Red Hen and two other restaurants worked together to set up a buffet lunch in front of the County Courthouse for the wake that followed the services. The crowds were large but quiet and respectful.

About 2:00, Tom and Jenelle went to the police station. There were calls to be made. While Tom called the dispatcher to thank all the other police and fire services for covering for them. Jenelle called the mayor's office. The phone rang just twice.

"Town Mayor's office, Judy speaking."

"Judy, this is Jenelle, is Mayor Thompson back from the wake yet?"

"Yes he is, Jenelle, and may I say you have my sympathy?"

"Thank you, Judy."

"I'll connect you."

"Hello, Jenelle, this is Jules Thompson."

"Hello Jules. Thank you for your kind words at the funeral this morning."

"You're very welcome, Jenelle. Mike was a great man, and we were privileged to have him as Fire Chief. There's no real replacing him."

"I know, John, but that's why I'm calling. I hope this call is not out of line."

"Go ahead."

"Mike and I talked many times about the men and women in his department. Mike told me about a year ago that if anything happened to him, that he hoped you would appoint Will Goodyear, at least as an interim."

"It's definitely not out of line, Jenelle. In fact, I called Will last evening and asked him to be our permanent Fire Chief."

"Really!"

"Yes. He's experienced. He's almost as decorated as Mike was, and in my estimation, he's got what it takes."

"I agree John. Thanks once more for your remarks this morning. We'll see one another again soon."

"Thanks for calling, Jenelle. Bye."

"Bye." As she hung up, she looked up and saw Tom standing in his office doorway. "Will is our new Fire Chief – permanently."

Mike nodded. "He's a good man." When you talk to him, have him give me a call. I'd like to buy him breakfast one morning."

"Will do. I'm scheduled for tomorrow off, but if you need me, I'd like to come in."

Tom smiled slightly. "I appreciate that, but you complained not too many weeks ago that you and Mike had gotten behind in your shared housework."

A tear rolled down her cheek. "I know. I'm not going to pack up Mike's belongings yet, but there are other things I can do."

"Right, and if you run out of chores, I can find some office work for you to do around here."

"Gee, thanks!" She wasn't smiling.

"You're welcome. Mom and Dad are staying with me through next weekend. I'm taking Sunday off. It's the first Sunday of December, and the music should be special. If you want to take Sunday morning off, we'll pick you up."

"I don't know yet."

"That's okay." He paused. "Do you know what is in that box in the corner of my office?"

"Not really. John Simpson from J & J Construction dropped it off. He said it was his way of saying thanks for treating his men and his company with respect."

Tom scowled and walked back into the office. He took the box to his desk, and he pulled out a small razor-sharp switchblade that he carried in his front pocket. Inside was a single-cup coffee maker, never used. He also found in the box a stainless-steel refillable brew basket, a bag of bulk Earl Grey tea, and a J & J Construction mug. For the first time in days, Tom smiled. "This will be a nice diversion," he muttered softly."

"What will be a diversion?" Jenelle came into his office. "Wow! All that was in the box?"

"Yep. This is to be for tea only, okay?"

"Absolutely! I love tea, although I don't drink Earl Grey every time. Mike and I...." Her voice trailed off, and Tom turned to look at her. "Mike and I had about a dozen different teas on the shelf, and I still do. I'll fill the reservoir if you'll plug it in and program it."

"It's a deal." Mike tossed his old water pot into the trash and plugged in the new brewer. He had just finished programming it when Jenelle came back in. "Thank you." He put the reservoir in place.

"Did it only come with one brew basket?"

Tom pointed to the box. "I think so, but take a look."

Jenelle rummaged through the packing materials, then said, "Victory! Here are two more! I've got a mug at my desk. You get the first mug of tea, and then I'll get one."

"It's a deal."

A few minutes later, they were sitting in his office drinking tea. Jenelle was thoughtful. This is better than any tea with a tea bag I've ever had." She paused. "I'm seeing a grief counselor this evening. I think you should too."

Tom nodded. "You're probably correct. You're definitely right that this is good tea. Do you mind my asking, who are you seeing?"

"Actually, I'm seeing Pastor Harold. Mike and I did not go to that church as you and Maria did. Did you know that he has a doctorate in counseling?"

He raised his eyebrows. "Really! I didn't know that."

"You know...."

"What?"

"If you say 'no' it's really okay, but I think it would help me if you went with me this evening just for the first session. We could tell him our story of the disaster together. It might feel good for both of us to talk it out. What do you think?"

Tom looked into his mug and then back up at her. "Yes. ... Okay. Even if it is of no help to me, if it helps you, then of course I'll go."

Jenelle half smiled. "Thank you. It's at 7:00 at the church."

"Okay."

As she got up, the phone rang. "I'll get that. You enjoy your tea."

"No, I've got it." He picked up the receiver. "This is Chief Kuster." He listened for about a minute. "No, thank you. I'll be fine. I appreciate the offer." He paused. "No, thank you. Bye." He hung up.

"Who was that?"

"Nothing important. What time is Jack coming in?"

"He's coming in at 2:30. He's got some paperwork to finish, and then he'll take the swing shift through the graveyard shift at his home. Why do you ask? Do you need something?"

"Perhaps. Bring your tea, and have a seat again."

She came and sat down. "What's up."

Tom spoke carefully. "I've prayed quite a bit about this. Mike and I shared a secret, and with him gone, I think that the Lord wants me to share it with you. If you don't want to keep a big secret for at least a few months, I won't share it with you."

Jenelle had her first smile in days. She leaned forward slightly "Tom, you and Mike were close, and for a long time, Mike and I have felt closer to you and Maria than anyone. I knew there was something going on, but I figured he would tell me eventually when he was ready. I saw a bill from the laboratory that the Fire Department uses that Mike paid cash for. It was an analysis for an air sample. Is this something about the cave with poison gas that Tommie discovered?"

Tom nodded. "When Jack comes in, take your patrol car and go east on the highway about a mile and a quarter. You'll see the old driveway marker that says 'Kuster.'"

"I know where it is, because it's the back door to the swimming hole. Will snow be a problem?"

He shook his head. "Naw. There are some snow and ice patches on the north side of some of some slopes, but there's no real problem. You'll see my truck by the swimming hole."

"This is beginning to sound like an adventure."

Tom raised his eyebrows. "I'm not sure how all of this is going to unfold, but I'm looking forward to having you along for the ride."

Jenelle looked at her watch. "Jack will be here in less than an hour."

"I'm going to go home and put a few things in my truck. When you meet me, have a pair of disposable gloves, safety glasses, and your favorite flashlight with two sets of fresh batteries." He got up and started for the door. "I'll see you in about an hour."

"Okay."

+ + +

As he drove home, the sky was clear and cold. Tom muttered to himself, "What am I doing? Why does this seem so right, yet so startling?" Leaving the patrol car in front, Tom walked to his garage. Into a knapsack he put a couple of extra battery packs for his spotlight, along with disposable gloves, AA cells, a couple of squeeze tubes of Rex-Hex glue, and an old D-Cell nightstick flashlight. He grabbed a couple of hard hats, a package of self-seal-able bags, and his tool belt. Then he stopped, thinking. He reached into a drawer and got a couple of high-intensity LED headlamps that he and Maria had used when night skiing. Stopping again, he reached up on a shelf and brought down a white disk about five inches in diameter. He put it in a pocket inside his coat.

Looking at his watch, Tom saw that he had another thirty minutes before Jenelle got there, so he went in the house. It was cool, dark, and smelled a little musty.

After turning up the thermostat, he went to the kitchen. He brewed himself a cup of English Breakfast Tea and grabbed an energy bar from a cupboard. Then he sat down in the living room. He put his tea on the table next to the recliner, leaned back, and bit into the energy bar. He could see Maria sitting in her rocker, and he saw the kids playing on the floor in front of the television.

As tears ran down his cheeks, he sat up straight, shook his head, and wiped his face against his sleeve.

Looking at his watch, Tom took a good swallow of tea, and he began to relax again. For just a moment he could see Jenelle sitting on the sofa, as she had with Mike many times. He got up and went back outside. Getting into the truck, the engine roared to life, and he drove quickly out the back road. Soon he saw Jenelle's patrol car parked by the swimming hole, and he pulled up beside her. She had changed out of her uniform into form-fitting black denim pants and a bulky knit red sweater. She also had a knapsack. "I see you changed. You look good!"

"Thanks! What's in the back?"

He pointed. "I don't know that we'll need all this, but we'd better be prepared. Put on one of those hard hats."" He reached into his knapsack and handed her a headlamp. "I think you'll find that handier than your usual flashlight. It's got fresh batteries, and there's more in my knapsack." He put on his tool belt, and hung his spotlight and old nightstick on it.

She handed him the other hard hat. "Where do we go?"

"Up there." He pointed at the boulders, and they began hiking. When they got close to the rocks, he veered left, and she followed.

When the plastic barrier with the warning stickers and police tape came into view, Jenelle said, "Wow. That looks impressive."

Tom nodded. "As it turns out, the barrier is not so much for safety but for security. If you read that report Mike got from the lab, you know that the methane concentration is extremely low – one hundredth of one percent. At least five percent is needed to be explosive."

"Okay, so why the need for security?"

"Mike and I saw two important things in here, but I think they are part of something much more important. From this day forwards, this is our private adventure together until we both decide otherwise. I'll first show you what Mike and I saw."

He reached for a utility knife on his belt and carefully slit the plastic near the right bottom corner.

"How are we going to re-seal it?"

"I've got Rex-Hex in my knapsack." He carefully slit some of the plastic away from the glue on the rocks to create a vertical loose flap. He grabbed the bottom corner of the plastic and folded it back. "Turn on your headlamp, then you can go first. You'll have to be stooped over for about fourteen to fifteen feet. When you can stand up straight, stop and wait for me."

"Okay." She crawled through the opening. With the light of her headlamp, she could see everything pretty well. It was almost a tunnel for about a dozen feet or so, and then she stood up. Her headlamp disappeared into the darkness, so she could only see the wall next to the little tunnel and Tom coming through it. "Where are we?" She saw him grab his spotlight, and then he reached into an inside pocket of his jacket and pulled out a disk and put it into a slot on the top of his spotlight.

"We're in a rather large cave that you'll see in a moment. I've put a high-temperature porous diffuser on the front of the spotlight, turning it into a small floodlight." He turned it on a slowly swung it from left to right."

At first, Jenelle was speechless. "Good Lord, this place is huge!"

He swung the light upward. "It's tall too!"

"This is amazing. Did I see a doorway directly across from us?"

"Yeah, we'll head that way in a minute. Come this way first." He started off to the right. "The floor's pretty smooth, but be careful."

"Right."

"Ah, here it is." He unclasped his nightstick from his tool belt. "Here, take this. It's a lot brighter than your headlamp. It's got an LED bulb I put in, to replace the original filament bulb."

She took it and turned it on. "Yeah, this is a lot brighter. You used to carry this around when you were on patrol?"

"Yeah, its hefty and tough, so it's pretty useful, though it's a little heavy." He started climbing steep stairs. "These rock stairs are crude, so be careful."

"Okay. I like this night stick."

"Good. It's yours. I don't use it anymore."

"Terrific! Thanks! You're right! These steps are steep. How far up are we going?"

"Only about fifteen feet. We're here." He offered her a hand, and as she stepped up they were on a platform about twenty feet wide a five feet deep. He swung his light around the cave. "Look. I took pictures when I was up here the first time, and I've got them in my office, but I thought you needed to see things from here first hand."

"Ummm. This is incredible. Did Mike come up here?"

"No, he went in the other direction from the tunnel. We met at the doorway on our right. Are you ready to go back down?"

"Yeah." She started back down. At the bottom of the stairs, she swung her night stick light up and down the wall. "Look at this!"

"Yeah. I think those are torch holes. They're all around the perimeter, and in the other room I saw. The only place where there are not any torch holes is a dozen feet or so either side of the tunnel." Mike started across towards the doorway, but Jenelle caught his arm. "Wait! Let's go around the perimeter the other side of the tunnel. Let's see what Mike saw. Maybe he missed something."

"Okay."

They moved a little faster as they walked the other perimeter. Jenelle led the way, shining her light up and down the wall as they went. "Wait! What's that?"

Tom pointed the flood directly at it. "It's hard to say. It's half-way up the wall. We'd need a really tall ladder or climbing gear to get up there and examine it."

"It's a window or portal of some kind."

Tom pointed the flood back towards the doorway. "Come on. We're more than three-quarters of the way around. You'll see that the wall surrounding the doorway is some kind of brick and not stone."

When they got to the door, Jenelle lightly brushed her hand down the jamb. "I see! Yes, it's masonry of some kind."

"Here, point your light at the flood. I'm going to change battery packs before we go through the door." Jenelle pointed the light downward, and Tom got another battery pack from his knapsack. When the flood came back on, he stood up and walked through the doorway. He aimed the flood at the cross on the right-hand wall.

Jenelle caught her breath. "Really! This is a chapel!"

"Point your light to those shelves on the right, and put on your disposable gloves."

"I've already got them on. "I see some books. Have you got some evidence bags?"

"They're in my knapsack. Help yourself. The books are probably very fragile."

"Right! I'll be careful." She opened his knapsack and took out some plastic bags. She closed it again. "I see two books. One is a little thicker." She put them in two separate bags and sealed them. She shined her light up and down the shelf. "Wait! There's a little door back here!" She reached in. "There's no latch, but the hinge is a bit stiff. I'll open it slowly." She peered in with her headlamp. "There're some larger books in here. I'll bet they're Bibles." Carefully, she put all of them in bags and put them in her knapsack."

"Is that kind of heavy?"

She smiled. "Yeah, but I can handle it."

"Okay. Come on over here." He walked towards the little cot. "Here, hold the flood. "I'll show you something." He handed her the flood. Slowly, he folded back the blanket, revealing the skeleton's head and shoulders.

"Wow! I wonder how old this is?"

"A couple hundred years, possibly more. Do you see the hood that frames the skull?"

Jenelle knelt down and examined it carefully. "Is that what the Roman Catholic priests call an alb?"

"I think so." He paused. "If we bring in the coroner to see this, it becomes something he has to put into his records, and I don't want that."

"What about my uncle? He'd love to get into this. We're talking both medicine and archeology now. What do you think?"

"Let's pray about it. I think we should take the books to Ruth Branch. I'll tell her that I can't tell her yet where I found them."

"Sounds like a plan. There's no rush on this skeleton."

"Right. Now, we may have a greater adventure."

"Where?"

"It's this way. I don't know if Mike noticed this other doorway or not, but I did. While Mike was checking out the skeleton, he had the fire department flood, so with my own flashlight, I did a quick turn around the perimeter of this chapel and made a little discovery. I forgot to mention it to Mike. Look!" Tom stepped through a small doorway, and Jenelle followed. He pointed. "There's a stairway to our right, and straight ahead is what looks like a pit, or...." He walked forward. "...a bathing pool, maybe?" Tom pointed the flood downward.

"Whoa! Do you see that?" She pointed the nightstick. "There's water flowing in...." she swung the light around, "...but I don't see where it goes out."

Tom unzipped his jacket and searched his inside pockets. He drew out a small vial. "Here! I thought I had one of these. It's a sterile vial."

"Good!" She took it from him, unscrewed the cap, stooped down, and filled it from the pool. Screwing on the cap again, she handed it to Tom. "Here. My knapsack is pretty full."

"Right. What do you think? Do you want to try going up those stairs?"

"Maybe very slowly and carefully. Those aren't stone, they're masonry." She moved towards the stairs. "I'm not nearly as heavy as you are. Maybe I should go first."

"I don't know..."

"I'll be okay."

"All right, but go very slowly and be careful."

"You've got that right." Jenelle took off her knapsack and put it on the floor. She put a foot on the first step, and then she gradually added her weight. "So far, so good." Another step, and she stopped to stand on it. She put a foot on the next step, and suddenly the stairs started crumbling. As she fell backward, Tom caught her easily. "Thanks! I'm glad you've got my back!"

"Always!" Tom put her down. "We've been in here a while now, and its probably dark outside. Let's call it a day, shall we?"

Jenelle nodded. "Agreed." She picked up her knapsack. "Let's go." As they walked across the big cave, she was thoughtful. "I've got some old catalogs that Mike ordered from. I'd have a hard time justifying borrowing a flood from the fire department, so I'm going to order one."

"That could be very helpful."

"I think before we come back we should get the books checked out and do some planning as to how to proceed. What do you think?"

"I agree. Ruth Branch at the library likes to work with rare books, so I'll take my mysterious find to her. He pointed the flood off to their right and upward. "I don't know how we can get up to that high opening without help from the fire department. I think we'll have to hold off on that adventure for a few months."

Jenelle nodded. "Right." She stooped down to go through the tunnel. When they got outside it was dark. She reached into Tom's knapsack and got the Rex-Hex glue. Jenelle quickly re-sealed the opening so that no one could see that they had been inside.

"Let's give some thought as to a better way to secure this cave rather than cutting our way in and gluing it back shut."

Jenelle nodded. "I agree. The last weather report I saw said that it was going to start snowing this weekend pretty heavily."

"I've been thinking about that." Tom paused. "Let's spend the next few months analyzing what we have so far and planning for returning in the Spring."

When they got down to the patrol car and truck, Jenelle handed Tom her knapsack. "Here, take it.

After you give Ruth the books tomorrow, you can leave it behind my desk."

"Okay. ... I'm hungry. I'd ask you to join me at the Little Red Hen, but we don't need to start gossip."

Jenelle giggled. "The mayor's secretary, Judy, would have a field day!"

Tom smiled. "That she would! I'm glad I brought you into this, Jenelle."

She nodded. "I am too."

"See you tomorrow." He smiled.

She looked into his face and smiled. "Tomorrow."

They drove off in opposite directions.

7.

Ruth Branch worked prolonged hours. Her husband, the resident physician at the hospital, also worked extensive hours. When they got married, she told him that she would work whenever he was working, and she would take time off when he did. That arrangement had been working for more than thirty years.

That particular morning, John had gone to the hospital early, so she dropped him off and went to The Little Red Hen for breakfast. As she walked in the door, she hung up her coat and scarf in the mud room. She went on in, and immediately she saw Tom Kuster, sitting in a corner by himself. She thought he must be lonely, so she crossed the café to greet him. "Good morning, Tom."

He looked up. "Good morning, Ruth. I'm glad to see you. Yesterday Effie told me that you almost always ate breakfast here, usually right after they open. Please join me."

Taken aback, Ruth hesitated. "Well, okay, thank you. This is a surprise."

Tom nodded. "I have some old books I'd like you to look at. In exchange, I'll buy you your breakfast. Would that be okay?"

"It's a bargain, Tom, but a café is not a good place to examine old books. Can you bring them to the library after we have breakfast?"

Tom smiled. "Of course."

Effie walked up. "Good morning, Ruth, Tom. What can I get you?"

Ruth looked up at her. "On this cold morning, I think I'll have cream of rice cereal, coffee, and a small orange juice."

"Good – and you, Tom?"

"I'll have eggs over easy with potatoes, turkey sausage, white toast, and Earl Grey."

"Got it." She quickly walked away.

"Tom, I must say, you have me curious. Did these books come from your basement?"

"Honestly, Ruth, no, but I cannot tell you where they come from at this time. I'm doing a quiet investigation, and I guess you can say that this is some unusual evidence in a mystery."

Ruth smiled. "I love a good mystery. It's nice to be part of one once in a while."

"Yes, you have a nice selection of mysteries at the library. I've read several of them."

"I've noticed. You seem to like both Perry Mason and Nero Wolfe mysteries."

Effie came with their tea, juice and coffee.

"Thank you, Effie." Tom took a sip of tea. "The Perry Mason mysteries I re-read once in a while because I liked them when I was a teenager. They're not nearly as well-written as the Rex Stout mysteries, particularly those about Nero Wolfe."

"Yes, Rex Stout was a prolific writer, increasingly so after he left the OSS at the end of World War II. Each of his mysteries can be enjoyed repeatedly. They're masterpieces of detective fiction." Ruth took a sip of coffee.

"I agree. I think one or two of these books I have for you are Bibles, but they're not in English. I hope you will be able to trace where they came from."

"You know already about the King James Version, dated, 1611. The oldest Spanish Bible was the Ferrara Bible, published in 1553. If it's Roman Catholic, the Vulgate was first translated late in the fourth century."

Tom nodded. "That's interesting. I have the books sealed in plastic bags. My signature and date are on each of the bags. When you open each bag, just sign and date when you opened them."

"Okay. I've dealt with evidence bags on other occasions. This will be an interesting diversion from my usual routine."

Effie then brought their food to them, and as they ate, they chatted about various subjects. After Tom paid the bill, Ruth drove her car to the library, and Tom followed in his patrol car. Going in, he carried the four books into the library in a locked leather briefcase Maria had given him several years earlier.

Ruth beckoned. "Come back here into my office and work area." The library's phone rang, and she picked it up. "Town Library, how can I help you?" She listened. "No, dear, I came straight here because Chief Kuster has some rare books that he wants me to examine." She paused a little longer. "6:30 will be fine. I'll see you there. Bye, dear." She hung up.

Tom set the briefcase on her large table and opened it. One by one, he removed the four sealed books and laid them out carefully. "That's all of them."

Ruth picked up the larger book closest to her. She thought a moment, then she got a large piece of butcher paper from a nearby dispenser, laid out the paper on the table, and laid the books on it. She looked at each of the larger books carefully through the plastic. "It appears that these two comprise a Vulgate Bible. The thicker one is the Old Testament and the other one is the New Testament."

Tom nodded. "I need to get to the station. There's no rush for me on these books, so please take your time. While I'm here, though, would you take a look at the smallest one? It has me very curious."

"Sure." She picked it up. She put her signature and date on a label on a sheet, peeled it off, and stuck it to the bag. Then she opened the bag and carefully took it out. "As dusty as it is, the binding appears to be in good condition, though fragile of course." She opened a drawer and put on some cotton gloves. She opened the cover carefully, and then turned a page. "Oh, my! This is a journal. It's written in Spanish. I'm looking for a date." She turned several pages. "Ah! June 16, 1764. This is very rare and valuable, Tom!"

Tom nodded. "Thank you, Ruth. Please learn as much as you can, and when you're finished, we can talk. In the meantime, this investigation is not for anyone else. We need to keep it confidential, okay?"

"She nodded. "I understand. I'll work on this when others are not around."

"Thank you, Ruth." Tom stood up, towering over her. I know we're getting close to Christmas, so I won't expect to hear from you until January or February, depending upon how much research you have to do."

"Thank you for trusting me with this. Will you be able to tell me where they came from?"

Tom nodded. "Eventually. I expect this investigation to go on for months. When I tell you where they came from, I'll probably give you permission to talk about it as much as you want to." He walked towards the door.

"Thank you for breakfast, Tom."

He turned and nodded. "Thank you for doing this, Ruth." He went out.

+ + +

The holidays were difficult for both Tom and Jenelle, but Pastor Gentle was a good counselor. Each of them had a session once a week through most of the winter. The weather was unusually cold, but it seemed to pass quickly as they kept themselves busy. Tom and Jenelle immersed themselves in work, and they began putting their sorrow behind them.

The first Monday morning in March, Tom was drinking his tea and reading some reports from the previous weekend. Jenelle came to the doorway. "Tom?"

He looked up from his reading and smiled. "What?"

"I've been looking again at the pictures that you took in December and shared with Mike."

"I've got my copies here in my bottom drawer." He pulled a folder out from under a stack of others. He put it on his desk.

She looked behind her to be sure they were alone. Turning back, she quietly said, "Look at the one you shot from the middle of the large cave towards the tunnel, the one that shows the area immediately above the tunnel opening."

Tom shuffled through them until he found it. After studying it for a moment, he looked up at her. "What are you talking about?"

She walked to his desk and pointed at an area just above the tunnel. "If there's enough megapixels in the image for decent resolution, can you blow up that area?"

"Sure!" He reached into his pocket and pulled out a thumb drive. He plugged it into his computer. As the software was opening it up, Tom said, "The camera has twenty megapixels of resolution, so it should be enough. As dark as it was, there may be some digital noise." He paused. "I think I see what you're talking about." He selected the area and sent it to the printer. "That color ink-jet is a little slow, so it'll be a minute or so."

"I know. I hope it shows what I think it will." She walked over to the printer, and as it released the page, she picked it up and showed it to him. "It's a little dark. Why don't you make a separate copy of that area and enhance it?"

"That should be easy." He went back to his computer and pasted the selected area as a separate image. Then he ran it through some high-end software that the department had purchased. A moment later, he said, "Whoa! I see what you mean. That could be the outline of the original cave opening before a slide covered it." They heard the front door of the station open.

She spoke softly. "When you get a moment, re-examine these pictures of the area surrounding the opening." She started out of his office. "I think I know where those rocks came from. I'll be happy to show you when we get a chance to do some more exploring."

"Good. Who came in?"

She craned her neck in the direction of her desk. "It's Jack."

Tom put away the folder, but he left the thumb drive in his computer. He called out, "Hey, Jack, come on in here a moment."

Jack came to the doorway. "Good morning, Chief. What's up?"

Tom pointed to a chair. "Have a seat. I read your report about J & J construction clearing their stuff out. Did they leave behind anything useful?"

Jack shook his head. "They did a very good job of cleaning up. I did tell road maintenance about the sand and gravel they left behind. They're going to haul it over to the edge of our quarry near the warehouse. They can always use sand for the roads during the winter."

Tom nodded. "Anything else?"

"Nope. ... Oh, wait! They left a non-functioning generator next to the temporary dumpster. I was surprised, because it doesn't look all that old."

"Is it on wheels?"

"Yeah."

"Interesting! Tell Will Smith at maintenance to check it out and see if it can be fixed. Towne has plenty of generators, but I wouldn't mind having one. Tell Will.... No, I'll call him. Why are you here this morning? You aren't due in until later."

"I left my thermos here the other day."

"Okay. I'll see you later then."

"Right. See you later." He left.

Flipping through his rotary card index, Tom found a number he needed. He punched in a number. "Hello, this is Chief Tom Kuster of the Towne Police Department. I've got a question about a piece of equipment your crew left behind last weekend."

"J & J's operator said, "Just a moment."

"John Simpson speaking."

"John, this is Chief Tom Kuster."

"Hey Chief. What can I do for you?"

"Your crew left a non-functioning generator by the dumpster."

"Yeah, I had to tinker with it constantly to keep it running while I was there. I decided to junk it. If you can fix it, you're welcome to it."

"That's great. It's got the J & J logo and serial number. Can you send me some paperwork, indicating it's no longer J & J property, to make things legal if it is fixed up?"

"Sure! No problem. That thing was a minor expense to the project. The last six weeks we were using another unit to keep the lights on."

"Thanks, John. By the way, as we're talking my deputy and I are drinking tea from that brewer unit you sent. Thanks again."

"Sure. Have a good day." The connection ended.

After hanging up, Tom punched another number. "Hey, Will, this is Chief Kuster."

"Hey, Chief! What's up?"

"I need a favor."

"Shoot."

"J & J left a generator unit behind when they left over the weekend. The last six weeks they used a different generator because this one was so unreliable. I know you've got plenty of generators over there. I'd like to have you tow it back to your place and see if it can be fixed. If so, see if you can convert it over to use natural gas. I'll pay you, whether or not you can fix it. Afterward, if it's useable, drop it off at my house."

"Okay." Will paused. "I can work on it this evening to see what's wrong. I'll let you know what has to be done."

"Great. I'll look forward to hearing from you. If I'm not home, leave a voice mail."

"Okay. Later." He hung up.

Turning to his computer, Tom pulled up the other pictures that Jenelle mentioned. He called out, "What are you working on, Jenelle?"

She came to the door. I'm filing last week's reports and working on the schedule for next month. Judy from the Mayor's office has offered to take me to lunch in about an hour. I'll be careful what I say to her."

Tom smiled. "Good idea. I'm looking at those pictures of the boulders you mentioned. I'm not seeing anything special."

Jenelle nodded. "I didn't either, at first. Zoom in on them, and notice the streaks of color in part of them." Tom worked his keyboard, while Jenelle came around to look over his shoulder. "There!" She pointed. "Do you see that streak? Do you remember seeing that pattern of color anywhere else?"

Tom cocked his head and closed his eyes. "Yeah, but where?"

Jenelle put her hand on Tom's shoulder. "I spotted it when J & J crews were working at the top of that hill, where the road curves north before going east again. They had to do some minor blasting."

"I think I know what you're talking about. It's near the edge of my property. When I go home later, I swing by and take a look. What do you think is the significance?"

Jenelle was thoughtful. "I'm not entirely sure. I don't know if you want to go to the expense, but you could bring in a geologist to check out the area. We can tell him about the cave but not tell him how big it is, and not show it to him because of the methane."

"Excellent idea. Dad had a geologist on the property a few years ago to see about a well. I can bring her back. She'll already be familiar with the general area. She may have consulted on the highway and bridge construction."

"Good. I'm going to get back to work and get as much done as I can before Judy gets here." She went out.

Tom spent the rest of the morning returning two phone calls from people telling him how donations he and Maria had sent out were being used. The checks that they had sent out just before she was killed had been greatly appreciated. He had been getting two or three such calls each week through the winter.

Then he called his Dad. "Good morning! This is Tom."

"Good morning! How are things out there?"

"Same old, same old, Dad."

"How's the grieving coming, Tom?"

"Both Jenelle and I have been seeing Pastor Harold, but I'm checking in with him less frequently. It's the same for Jenelle. I've got a question. Do you remember bringing in a geologist several years ago to survey our property?"

"Sure. Let me think. ... That was Mandy Huggins. She lives in Stockton now. Is this about the cave?"

"Kind of. I'll be able to tell you and Mom a lot about it when you come for Easter."

"Good. I'll have your Mom send you an email with Mandy's address and phone. She's nodding at me and pointing at our computer, so I guess she's going to send it to you right now."

"Good, Dad. Tell Mom I'm really looking forward to seeing you two for Easter. If you're here for the previous Thursday, there's a special communion service at Towne Community Church."

"We'll make it a point to be there. Is your freezer working okay?"

"Sure, why do you ask?"

"Your Mom wants to fill it with bread and pastries while she's there."

"That sounds great! Give her my best. I've got to go. I'll call you next weekend. I love you!"

"We love you too, son. Bye." The connection ended.

Tom heard noises in the outer office. Jenelle called out, "Judy and I are going to lunch. We'll be back in an hour."

"Okay, enjoy your lunch."

Tom turned to his computer and checked his email. There was one from his Mom. Opening it, he read it through, smiling. He wrote down the information about Mandy Huggins on his scratch pad, then he punched in her number.

It rang twice, and then he heard, "Hello?"

"Mandy Huggins?"

"Yes."

"This is Tom Kuster, Mike and Trina Kuster's son."

She hesitated. "Oh, yes, you're over in Towne, that little burg in the Sierra foothills. That was several years ago. What can I do for you?"

"It's kind of complicated. My wife and family were killed when a train derailed in early December."

"I'm so sorry! I read about that derailment and explosion. Your family was in that van?"

"Yes, and two firemen were killed in the hydrogen explosion. Anyway, my son discovered a cave on our property just before he was killed. He was very interested in knowing all about it. I've sealed the small entrance due to the presence of methane gas. Tommie wanted to know why this cave appeared at that time. We thought it might have been because of a recent tremor. There's also been highway construction nearby because they widened the roadbed and built a new bridge near Towne."

"I see. How much investigating do you want done? I did some consultations for the highway construction. That's standard procedure. I also helped with planning for the foundation of the new bridge."

"Interesting! I have a little money available, so I'm not putting a budget limit on it yet. Let's take it step by step. How soon can you get started?"

"Well, I just completed a survey up north near the Oregon border. I can start right away."

"Great! If you need me to sign a contract, I'm the Chief of Police, so just bring the paperwork to the police station."

"Okay. I can be there by Wednesday."

"Good. See you then."

"Bye."

Tom hung up, and then he picked up the receiver and punched in another number. "Hello, Ruth, this is Tom Kuster."

"Hello, Tom. I meant to call you last week, but I forgot. All four of the books are dated the second half of the eighteenth century. The two bigger ones comprise a Bible, as I thought. The smallest is a journal by a priest who was associated with Junipero Serra. His name was Francisco Palóu."

"Very interesting. What about the other book?"

"I found it a bit more of a challenge at first. It is a Spanish reader, designed to help educate Native Americans I think. I should have asked you, but I enlisted the help of the Spanish teacher at our high school. He's new. His name is Jim Chabert. I like him. He helped me with both the journal and the reader. He's keeping it all under his hat, because I told him that the books were part of an investigation by our Police Chief. When am I going to learn more about the source of these books, Tom?"

"As it stands now, I'm thinking I will be able to tell you at the end of the summer. How's that?"

"I'll be looking forward to it. Meanwhile, I'm keeping the books in the library safe. I won't be looking at them again until an archivist friend of mine gets here in a couple of weeks. With your permission, she will give each of them a condition rating and an approximate value." She paused. "Someone has come in. I have to go, Chief."

"Okay. Go ahead with that archivist. Thank you, Ruth."

"You're welcome."

Tom sat back in his chair and finished a mug of tea that had grown cold. He heard the front door open and Jenelle's voice. "I'm back!"

"Good! I'm hungry! How was lunch?"

"Delicious! The Little Red Hen has a special kind of German roast beef today. It's called sauerbraten. It's tender and wonderful."

Tom got up from his desk. "I'll have to try it. Before I go, a geologist named Mandy Huggins will be arriving Wednesday. She'll probably have paperwork for me to sign." He lowered his voice slightly. "I talked to Ruth Branch, and she's going to bring in an archivist to rate and value the books. They're all from the second half of the eighteenth century. In addition to the Vulgate Bible volumes, there's a reader for teaching Native Americans, and the journal belonged to Francisco Palóu. You might want to look him up on the Internet. ... See you in about an hour." He headed out the door.

8.

It was the second Saturday in March, and when Tom awakened, he automatically reached across to the empty side of the bed. Remembering he had the day off, he turned over to go back to sleep. Suddenly, his cell phone rang. It was on his dresser on the other side of the room, so he scrambled out of bed.

As he reached for the phone, he glanced at the clock. 7:30. He rubbed his eyes as he answered. "Hello?"

"Tom? You don't sound like you!" Jenelle's voice made him suddenly wide awake."

"Good morning! I overslept. What's wrong?"

"Nothing's wrong, but you never oversleep. You're always awake by 5:00 and in the office before 6:00."

"It's my scheduled day off unless …. What's going on?"

"Charly traded shifts with me on Thursday, so he's got my shift today. I've got something for the cave for us to play with. Do you want to come out and play?"

Tom chuckled. *What a woman*, he thought. "Sure! How soon?"

"I can meet you there in thirty minutes."

"Cool! It's a date!" *Why did I say that?* He thought.

"See ya there." Jenelle ended the call.

Tom stared at the clock, shook his head, and headed to the bathroom.

Fifteen minutes later, Tom went out the back door with a spill-proof mug of tea in his right hand and a toasted pastry in his left. He stuffed the last of the pastry into his mouth before opening the garage door. He looked up into the sky, which was clear, and

Spring seemed to be in the air, though the calendar said it was still more than a week away. As he drove past his garage on his way into the forest, he saw the generator parked behind the building. "Nice," he muttered. "I'll have to talk to Will on Monday."

He drove rapidly, and Jenelle was waiting for him in her little Subaru wagon. He looked at his watch, and they were both right on time. As he got out, he said, "Good morning again!" and held out his arms. They hugged, and then he looked into her eyes. "So what have you brought that we're going to play with? You've got me curious."

She pointed. "It's on the roof of my car. It's not as heavy as it looks." She went over to her car and pulled back a tarp, revealing what appeared to be a rough slice of a boulder. She reached up and touched it. "Feel it! It's made to look and feel like granite. The whole thing weighs less than a hundred pounds, and it has hinge pins and a latch loop. I've got the rest in the car."

He touched it. "What gave you this idea?"

Jenelle smiled. "I was in that remodeling store at the mall on Presidents' Day, and I saw the area where they had artificial stone counter tops. It was a special order, but it took less than a month to make."

Tom grinned. "I like it. Let's drag it up the hill with the curve side down so we scuff it up a bit."

They gathered up their gear, and then they fastened a rope to the hinge pins. They dragged it behind them as they made their way up the slope to the boulders.

As they moved, Tom remarked, "Will Smith finished repairing my generator I got from J & J. It's sitting behind my garage. Will says it has a twenty-five kilowatt capacity."

"Good." She puffed, "This fake boulder seems to be getting heavier. ... Where do you plan to install the generator?"

They reached the boulders, so they stopped, and he pointed. "I want to put it into the hillside a bit below us and above the swimming hole. It will be a berm shed, with three sides buried into the hillside. The bottom side will be an aluminum gate with heavy security mesh."

Jenelle nodded. "That sounds good. It will be nice to have lights for the swimming hole on hot summer evenings. You and I can run the separate and secret conduit up the hill so that we have lighting available in the cave. It shouldn't be too hard. Later, other circuits can be added."

Tom smiled. "I've already talked to an electrician, Dave Moore, and there'll be lots of underwater LED lights. He said I have too much generator capacity for the lights in the lake, but I did not tell him about supplying power to the cave yet. We'll have him do that after we go public with Tommie's cave."

"Why not call it that?"

"What?"

"Why not call it 'Tommie's Cave."

Tom grinned. "I like that! We can also name 'Maria's Chapel, 'Mike's Motel,' 'Alice's Lookout,' and 'Karen's Pool.'"

Jenelle shook her head. "I think I can come up with a better name than 'Mike's Motel' for the sleeping quarters." I'll think about the other labels too."

"Good idea. I was just thinking of those ideas off the top of my head." He looked around. "It may not be officially Spring yet, but we have an entire beautiful day to get some things done."

"Right. What do you say we get rid of the barrier and install our new rock?"

"That's a good start."

About four hours later, they were sitting beside the lake and sharing a picnic lunch that Jenelle had packed, along with a large thermos of tea. Jenelle pointed at the lake. "How deep is Dave Moore going to put the lights?"

Tom chewed a bite of sandwich and swallowed. "About ten feet from the shore there'll be a string of lights spaced five to six feet apart, the entire length of the lake, from the spring inlet on the south end to the dam's overflow at the north end. They'll be on this side only because nobody goes to the other side due to the brush and irregular bottom. Believe it or not, the total power consumption for that string will be less than ten amps."

"That will be pretty at night."

"Yeah." He paused. "There'll be a second string of lights about twenty-five feet out on another circuit. Those lights will have twice the brightness, but they'll look about the same as the others due to the depth." Jenelle started to speak, but he continued. "In the middle of the lake there'll be a higher wattage array of lights bright enough by itself to give light to the whole lake. It will be on a third circuit."

"Wow! That sounds great! Won't all this be kind of expensive?"

Tom shook his head. "Not really. The state paid Maria and I a nice chunk of change for the land they took from us when they widened the highway. It will cover the cost of both these lights and any in the cave we install."

Jenelle reached for the thermos. "Do you want a refill?"

He smiled. "Sure!"

She filled his cup. "Is the generator gas or diesel? You're going to need to bury a tank, won't you?"

Mike shook his head. "No. I had Will convert the engine to natural gas. Our main Towne gas line comes into the area just the other side of the lake. There's a cutoff valve and junction about three hundred yards from here. There's a line going to my house and those of my neighbors from that junction. I've told Sammy's plumbing that I'm going to need a gas line to this area of the lake soon."

"It sounds like you've been doing a lot under cover, Tom. If you're done with your tea, let's get in my car and go up to the top of the hill. I've read what Mandy Huggins reported to you. I've also read some old newspaper articles about a rock slide in 1811. I think I've figured out how the cave got to be the way it now is."

Tom nodded. "I haven't had a chance to read Mandy's report yet. Let's go up and see what you've got. He got up, and he gave her a hand getting up. They gathered up the remnants of their picnic and got into her wagon. It only took about five minutes to go down the road to the highway, and then up the highway to the new scenic overlook that J & J installed.

Going over to the perimeter safety wall, Jenelle pointed downward. "Directly below us, above the construction debris, is a drop-off of about twelve feet. I took a tape last Thursday and did some measuring." She turned and faced him. "Based on the newspaper articles, a slab of rock about thirty yards wide, eleven feet tall, and twenty yards deep slid off the top of the hill, moving almost due west. The newspapers said it was because of an earthquake. According to Mandy, the boulders directly in front of the cave are not of the same composition as the slab that went down from here. Mandy says that the boulders are probably what is left of a rock formation that brought the slab to a halt."

Tom nodded. "This all makes sense. Did Mandy say why she thought the cave was uncovered?"

"I asked her that on the phone after she left, and I had read her report. She said she could not be sure, but the slab was probably weakened where it came to a stop at those boulders. She said she wished she could have seen inside the cave, but I told her that you as Police Chief and Mike as Fire Chief had labeled it as dangerous. She went on to say that earthquakes over a period of time, coupled with erosion, probably continued to weaken the area, until the opening appeared. I've noticed, when we walk the tunnel, that it is made mostly of large and irregular chunks of rock."

Tom nodded. "That also makes sense." He paused. The cave is even more secure, now that we've installed that camouflage rock. "I've got a crew coming on Monday to start building the berm enclosure for the generator. After you drop me off at my truck, why don't you go home? You've got Shultz and Sons coming to service your furnace this afternoon, don't you?"

Jenelle nodded. "Right. I think they're going to give me a new thermostat as well as change the filters. Let's get going."

As they drove down, Tom asked, "My waking nightmares have stopped. Have you stopped dreaming about the disaster?"

Jenelle nodded. "Yes. I thought about that when I was driving home from seeing Pastor Gentle last week. I don't think I need to go back to him."

"I'm the same. We'll never forget, but we're moving on, aren't we." Tom looked at her.

She brought her wagon to a stop beside his truck. "Tom, this cave project has been good for me, and you've been wonderfully good to me. Thank you."

She leaned over and kissed him on the cheek. "We'd better get going."

Tom smiled. "You've been very very good for me as well. I owe you a lot." He opened the door, got out, and got into his truck. They waved at each other just before she drove away. Tom turned his truck around and went home.

+ + +

Two weeks later, Tom and Jenelle were standing next to the generator's enclosure. It was nearly twice the size of the generator itself because of soundproofing. Lifting up a small cover just under the roof's overhang, he inserted a key and turned. They could hear a quiet hum as the generator started. Jenelle turned to look at the lake.

Tom shook his head. "The lights under the lake are not coming on because they're on a photo sensor. Since it's the middle of the afternoon, I doubt we'd be able to see much of them right now anyway. I'm just turning on the power to the cave."

Jenelle's eyes got wider. "There's already power in the cave?"

Tom nodded. "It's all according to code. I did it myself during this past week for less than a hundred dollars. I've mounted a box just inside the main cave. For now, there's just four outlets and one twenty amp circuit. More can be added later of course."

"Is there light in there yet?"

He nodded. "Last month, I bought an HID floodlight. Tommie had a portable basketball hoop on a pole, so I took the hoop and backstop off and mounted the floodlight. It's wired with a cord and plug, and it's connected to one of the outlets in the cave. I've got a thousand watts of floodlight aimed at the ceiling."

They made their way up the hill. As Tom reached under a rock and released a catch, he swung the cave's "boulder" cover open. Jenelle peered into the darkness. "I think we need to see if we can enlarge this opening."

Tom nodded. "I agree. As I was burying the conduit, I've thought about that, but I don't see any worry-free solution. We've had it easy so far."

They went in. As they stood up, Jenelle heard the click of a switch Tom had mounted on the pole. The cave began to glow. "Cool," was all she could think of to say.

"Yeah! It takes a few minutes for the light to warm up and get to full intensity." They stood there and watched. As the ceiling became more well-lit, shadows began to form all around the perimeter of the cave from the irregular rocks.

Jenelle took off her backpack, reached inside, and took out a toy rifle. "There's something I'm curious about, and I think this may help us solve a little mystery."

"Another one?"

"In a way. We've wondered about how they got up to that opening high up on the wall. You named it "Alice's look out.""

Tom smiled. "It does kind of look like a window."

"I agree, but I think it's a natural opening." This toy rifle is supposed to fire rubber balls, but it's also just the right diameter to fire a badminton shuttlecock."

Tom raised his eyebrows. "Why here?"

"You'll see." Jenelle inserted a shuttlecock and pumped up the pressure in the toy. She walked over close to the wall underneath "Alice's look out."" She pointed the toy rifle straight up, in front of the opening high above.

When she fired and the shuttlecock reached the opening, it suddenly flew into an arc toward Tom and landed at his feet. "Whoa! That's not a window, it's a vent! What made you think of this? That's incredible!"

Jenelle was laughing. "I wasn't sure that would work!"

He started laughing too. "There's evidently more than one opening to this cave."

Still smiling, she explained, "I was lying in bed one night, remembering things Mike had told me, and I remembered him telling me about setting up exhaust fans in a house when there was a gas leak. That made me think of the air sample taken in the chapel area, how it contained a trace of methane. That, in turn, got me to thinking that the air always smells fresh here in the main cave. In my mind, I pictured the high opening, and that led me to picturing the opening and whether it could be a natural vent. Now we know that fresh air is coming in, and there are probably other vents we just don't see."

"By the way, the water in the pool is as pure as the water coming from the spring near the swimming hole. I am now convinced that this was, in fact, an undocumented mission of some kind." Tom started walking toward the chapel, and she followed. Tom pointed his spotlight up the stairs. "I don't think we should consider going to an upper level until we involve more people in this effort, do you?"

"No." Jenelle was adamant. "I think we should start by bringing Mandy Huggins back to examine the cave more thoroughly for stability of the whole area. It looks like this mission was small, but we may never know why."

"I agree." Tom turned. Before we go, let's look at the entrance more carefully, now that we have better light on the inside."

"Good idea." They started walking across the main cave. She asked, "When are your parents getting here for Easter?"

"I think they'll get here in time for lunch on Maundy Thursday. I'll be on duty all day. I'd like to have you join us in church in the evening. There's a special communion service."

"I'd like that. I'm on call that night, so I'll just turn down the volume on my radio and cell." She looked up at the wall above the tunnel. "Let's break out a tape and measure the width of this area between the tunnel and the curve of the ceiling."

"Right." Tom unclasped a tape measure from his tool belt. "Here, take the end, and go down to the place where the curve of the ceiling touches the floor. I'll do the same in this direction."

When she got there, she called out, "Okay! How many feet?"

Tom called out, "Thirty-four! Let go of your end." Cranking in the tape and walking towards the tunnel, he said, "That's wider than I thought. It looks like the tunnel is slightly off center to our left. There's no reason it would have to be centered, of course."

"I agree. Let's leave the light on and turn it off later at the generator. Let's also measure the same distances around the tunnel on the outside."

He nodded. "Good. Let's go. Have we got everything?"

"Yeah. Let's go." She stooped over and went out.

When they got outside, Tom got a couple of small cans of spray paint out of his backpack. "Let's go above the tunnel, put a mark there on that tree," he pointed, "and then measure out the width and mark a rock or tree at each end."

Jenelle nodded. "Sounds like a plan."

It did not take long to make the marks. Then they headed back down the hill. The sun was getting close to the horizon. When they got to the generator hut, Tom turned off the cave's circuit, and the hum of the generator stopped. He turned to Jenelle, saying, "I'll call Mandy Huggins when I get in tomorrow morning. I'll tell her that we want to keep all this confidential for a couple of more months. Do you know any archeologists?"

Jenelle shook her head. "No. We'll have to pray about finding one. I'm going to be a little later tomorrow morning. I'm getting my teeth cleaned."

"Okay." They hugged. He winked. "I'll see you tomorrow."

"Good night." She smiled.

+ + +

After church and after dinner on Easter Sunday, Tom and Jenelle sat around the table with his folks having cherry pie. Tom looked at his Dad. "When we were at the zoo some months ago, I told you that after Easter, I hoped to clear up a mystery for you and Mom."

Mike Kuster nodded. "I remember. It was while we were watching one of the shows."

"Right. Last Fall, Tommie discovered an opening to a cave on the hill above the swimming hole."

Tricia nodded. "I remember you telling us that it was sealed because of methane gas."

"That's right Mom, but Mike and I did not tell the entire story to anyone. When Maria and the kids were killed, and Jenelle's husband, Mike, was also killed with another fireman, I alone was left knowing the complete story. After more than a little prayer, I knew that Jenelle should know what Mike and I discovered."

Jenelle smiled. "It was the best thing that Tom could possibly have done for me and for the both of us."

Tom returned her smile. "Yes, we've been good for each other, and there's much more to tell about the cave. It is a previously undocumented eighteenth-century mission."

"Really!" Both his parents exclaimed.

Jenelle nodded. "The outer cave is about fifty yards wide and thirty yards deep, with a ceiling of at least fifty feet. Small traces of methane are further inside in other rooms."

Like flood waters released, Tom and Jenelle told his parents all they knew about the cave. The discussion went through the rest of the afternoon and into the evening. Finally, Jenelle said, "I'm on duty tomorrow morning, so I'd better get some rest." She stood up and gave hugs to Tricia and Mike, and then Tom walked her out the door onto the porch. "Tom, this has been an Easter I will never forget." She hugged him.

Tom put his finger under her chin, tilted her face upward, and kissed her briefly. Jenelle put her arms around his neck, pulled him downward, and kissed him back. Mike and Tricia watched them from the doorway.

9.

That week, Tom led Mandy Huggins into the cave, and Jenelle followed them. As Mandy stood up in the cave, her mouth hung open. "Fascinating! This is simply fascinating. This is so much bigger than I pictured in my mind."

Jenelle stood up next to her. "It's kind of pretty in its own way, isn't it?"

"Oh, yes. Definitely." Mandy walked around the perimeter, sometimes stopping to chip off a sample and put it in a bag. She labeled each sample carefully. Looking across, she saw the opening high up on the wall. "I would guess that's a vent, larger than the others."

Tom walked over. "The others?"

"O, yes." She pointed to several places. "The cracks there ... and there ... and there probably function as vents. This one," she pointed, "is a small vent. Hold your hand next to it, and you'll feel a slight draft. I love caving!" She stopped where the texture of the wall changed. "Ooh. This isn't natural."

"No," said Jenelle, "they're part of an interior wall made of substantial bricks. That sizable opening high up is a vent, as you said. We've tested it with a shuttlecock fired from a toy air rifle."

Mandy smiled. "Interesting...." Going past the doorway deeper into the hill, she remarked, "You can call me back after archeologists have examined this area if necessary." She continued walking the perimeter, taking samples. When she got back to the tunnel, she stepped backward from the wall several paces. You can enlarge this tunnel to a user-friendly size using non-explosive demolition agents."

Tom approached her. "I did not know there was such a thing."

"Oh, yes, they're quite common. Do you remember John Simpson from J & J Construction?"

"Yes, he seems to be a good man."

"That he is. When he was building the new bridge about two miles from here, I was his geologist on call. John is a certified demolition engineer."

Jenelle nodded. "I don't remember that company using dynamite. Was he using non-explosive agents?"

"Correct, but in a couple of cases, he also used dynamite. If you decide to use his services, tell him to call me. I'll give him some guidelines. Meanwhile, I'll keep all this confidential until you tell me otherwise, Tom."

"Good." They all went out.

Down by their vehicles, Tom turned off the cave lights. "Thank you, Mandy, for your time and expertise. Please send your bill to me at my house."

"Okay. She pointed across the lake. "Will you listen to some free advice?"

Tom grinned. "Always! I can't promise I'll take it, though."

Mandy nodded and smiled. "Understood. That dam your Dad built many years ago has problems. I looked at it last year when I was surveying for the highway. The dam might not hold beyond next winter. If it gives way suddenly, Towne could have a serious flood event, and worst-case scenario, it could close the highway temporarily. There's a relatively easy solution."

Tom was very serious. "Go on."

"A crane can put a pre-fabricated culvert with a built-in water gate just above the dam. Those pre-fab units are about three meters long and two meters wide. Then you bury it, creating a controlled and permanent earth berm dam."

Tom nodded. "I understand. Thank you."

"You're welcome. You'll get my bill for examining the cave in a week to ten days." She went to her car, climbed in, and rolled down her window. "It's been nice working with you. If you need me again, just call."

Jenelle smiled. "Thank you, Mandy. God bless you!"

"Thanks." The geologist drove off.

Tom walked slowly toward the edge of the lake, and he stared out over the water. Jenelle followed him down, put her arm around him, and looked up at him. When she put her arm around him, he put his arm around her, but he continued to look out over the water. Jenelle squeezed him. "Are you thinking about what Mandy said about the dam?"

Tom blinked. "I guess. No, actually I'm not. Something's nagging at the back of my mind, and I'm not sure what it is."

"Does it have to do with the cave?"

Tom looked at her. "This is going to seem like an off-the-wall question maybe, but ... when Cappy and Charlyn were filling in for us in January, you and Charlyn seemed to hit off pretty well."

Jenelle blinked. "Off the wall is right." She stopped to think. "Yeah, her sister was killed two years ago, so she was a supportive friend who could talk with me as one who's been there, sort of. Why do you ask?"

"Let's make an unofficial request for a favor."

"What?"

"Ask her if she or Cappy can check the CHP file on J & J. Have them see what they have on John Simpson."

"That's easy." Jenelle took out her cell phone and dialed. "Hi, Charly, it's Jenelle. ... I'm fine. Tom and I would like to ask an unofficial favor – something off the record. I'll put this on the speaker." She pushed a button and held the phone between them."

"Okay."

Tom looked at Jenelle and then at the phone. "Charlyn, this is Tom Kuster, and I want to emphasize this is unofficial."

"Okay."

"I assume that the CHP has a file on J & J Construction."

"Probably. I'm at my station. Let me get to a computer. Hold on a minute." There was some rustling in the background. "Okay. Is there anything or anyone, in particular, you want to check on?"

"A man named John Simpson."

"Simpson. ... John. ... He's been with the company for about fifteen years. ... He's a highway construction supervisor and a consultant in demolition. ... No complaints. ... Here's an interesting item. Two years ago, he requested a background on a geologist named Mandy Huggins, who lives way up north. Oh! I remember her! I met her a few months ago. She was with him at Bill's Bar and Grill. It looked like they could possibly be an item."

Jenelle winked at Tom. "Thanks, Charlyn, so you don't see anything negative there about John Simpson?"

"No."

Tom nodded. "Thanks Charlyn! We owe you one. Give my best to Cappy."

"Glad I could help. Take care." The phone went silent."

Jenelle looked at Tom. "What brought that on?"

Tom smiled. "Didn't you notice how Mandy's tone of voice changed when she was talking about John Simpson?"

Jenelle thought a moment. "Now that you mention it, her voice did change a little."

Tom nodded. "They may not be an item but just friends. That's not the issue. We've learned to trust

Mandy's expertise, so this makes it easier to trust John when having him look at the cave." He paused. "The ground's kind of wet, and there's no place to sit here. Let's sit on my truck's tailgate."

The western sky was turning pink as the sun got lower on the horizon. They went to the truck, and Tom pulled down the gate. As they sat down, he took out his cell phone and scrolled through his directory. He touched the screen a few more times. Holding the phone, he rested his wrist on Jenelle's knee.

"Hello?"

"John? This is Tom Kuster from Towne."

"Hey Tom! How are ya?"

"Fine. If you don't mind my asking, where are you working today?"

"I'm home, taking a day off. Yesterday I finished a job up near the little town of Weed. I've nothing more major scheduled this month except a couple of consultations. Why do you ask?"

"I was talking with Mandy Huggins today. She tells me you're a demolition engineer, and she talked about non-explosive demolition. I've got a job on my property here that I'd like you to consider."

"What's the details?"

"Mandy seemed to know you pretty well, and she knows all the details from her perspective as a geologist. She's expecting to hear from you, I think."

"Okay. She's a fine woman. I've worked with her several times."

"Good. Can you come by the Towne Police Station tomorrow?"

"Sure. I'll be there about 9:00."

"Great! See you then."

Closing the phone, Tom was thoughtful. He looked at Jenelle. "I noticed last week that you're no longer wearing your wedding set."

"You took off your band about two weeks ago."

"Yeah. I needed to in order to move on." He reached into his jacket. "Maria did not like to wear jewelry." He opened a green velvet box. "This ring has been in the Kuster family for at least four generations." He looked at her.

Jenelle's eyes got big. "It's beautiful!" She looked at him and then kissed him.

"Jenelle, will you marry me?"

"Yes!" Tears rolled down her cheeks. "Yes! Yes! Yes!" She kissed him again, but longer.

Tom was very serious. "You loved Mike totally and completely, and I loved Maria totally and completely, but I've always felt bonded to you, somehow."

She nodded. "I've felt the same bond. When we were grieving, I felt a little guilty about my feelings for you, but I talked to Pastor Gentle about it, and he said it was completely normal."

Tom laughed. "I told him the same thing. It could be he has been waiting to hear from us."

They laughed, and then they held each other a long time.

"You know...." Jenelle was smiling.

"What?"

"We both had big formal weddings the first time. I don't need that again."

Tom grinned. "I don't either. Who do you want to stand up for you?"

"I think I told you and Maria once that my parents died in an auto accident eleven years go. My sister Abby is the only family I have left except for some distant cousins. She's going to be here Friday and Saturday. It's the first time I've seen her in three years."

"Do you think she can stay through Sunday morning?"

"What do you have in mind?"

"Call Pastor Gentle, and ask him if he would like to preach a sermon on love on Sunday morning, and conclude it with marrying us. Tell him it's a secret until he calls us forward."

"Wow! Sounds like fun!"

"If he agrees to do it, I'll invite my parents to spend the weekend here. We don't need a reception. We'll leave after church for a short honeymoon. We can juggle the schedule so that Jack and Charly cover for us through Wednesday. I'll pay them the overtime out of my own pocket." Jenelle through her arms around Tom, and they kissed and continued to kiss long after the setting of the sun.

The next few days were almost frantic with activity. In a confidential conversation with a realtor friend who had been her roommate in college, Jenelle arranged for her house to go up for sale the following Monday. She made several trips between her house and Tom's during the evenings. She boxed up Maria's clothing, and she and Tom put it in the attic. They decided that the children's clothing could wait until after the honeymoon.

There were no tears shed. Both had moved on. After packing a suitcase for the honeymoon, they decided that movers could move the rest. It was exhausting but fun for both. They had to tell Jack and Charly when they changed the schedule for the next week. They agreed to keep the secret.

Friday morning, Tom was reading the mail when Jenelle came in. "Good morning, love."

"Good morning, my bride!"

She leaned down and kissed him. "Shhh! Not too loud!" she smiled. She went to the table and brewed a cup of tea. After adding sugar, she walked over and sat down on his desk. "How'd it go with John Simpson?"

Tom chuckled. "It was interesting! I hope those two are not having an affair. I stood by while they talked a lot of technical stuff, and then he summarized. He's going to pre-fabricate a tunnel with lots of steel re-enforcement. He'll use non-explosive demolition agents to clear just enough away to slide in the tunnel. Then they'll re-enforce the hill on the outside with steel and shotcrete. On the inside, the tunnel should barely protrude into the cave. The bottom side of the tunnel will include runner spaces for utilities as needed."

"Sounds like a neat installation."

"Yes. On the outside will be steel-clad doors with heavy duty locking mechanisms for security. We also talked about the dam. John will fix it up with the same crew and treat it all as one job, but in two phases."

Jenelle nodded. "I took Dave Moore aside at a job he's working on over at the Dimple's house. He'll pull out your temporary circuit and put in four twenty-amp circuits. I gave him a full tour of the cave early this morning. He's going to look at some catalogs and suggest some lighting to you at the end of next week."

Tom nodded. "That's great, dear." He put the mail down. My parents will get here this afternoon. Dad said they saw us kiss on Easter Sunday, and they've kind of been expecting all this."

Jenelle smiled. "How long will they be able to stay?"

"Mom promised they will be gone before we get home on Wednesday. They're going to supervise getting your stuff moved in. They've known the owners of Sierra Hills Moving and Storage since high school days. Robin and Julie don't do any of the labor anymore, but they supervise and keep the books for their children."

Tom winked. "We can enjoy our honeymoon without a thought about what's going on in Towne."

Jenelle grinned. "Absolutely!"

+ + +

On Sunday morning at Towne Community Church, nothing seemed out of the ordinary except that Tom and Jenelle were there on the same day, and Tom was wearing a suit and tie. Neither of them displayed any nervousness. Previously, one of them was almost always on duty. Toward the end of the sermon, on a secret signal from the pastor, Tom got out of his pew and went to stand by a door near the front while the pastor continued what he was saying. Jenelle already left at the beginning of the sermon to get ready.

Exactly as planned, the piano player started playing Richard Wagner's "Bridal Chorus," Tom walked to the center, and his father joined him. Jenelle's sister, Abby, walked down the center aisle, followed by Jenelle. She had changed into a bridal gown that she had rented for the day, and it accentuated her figure. Her flaming red hair hung loose down her back, just as it had when she had won the Miss Texas title. She was absolutely stunning. There was murmuring throughout the congregation.

When Pastor Gentle pronounced them husband and wife, there was applause and a few whistles as they kissed.

They turned toward the congregation, and Tom held up a hand. Everyone got quiet. "Jenelle was madly in love with Mike, and I was madly in love with Maria, but over the last seven months, we've both moved on. Our previous weddings were big events, but this one is small."

Jenelle grinned. "This is not traditional, but Tom and I are not even going to join you for the coffee hour. We're leaving for our honeymoon in Monterrey just as soon as we can change clothes. We want to thank you all for sharing this special day with us."

They both waved, and they quickly went through a side door into the pastor's office, where they had their other clothes. As Pastor Gentle pronounced a closing prayer, Abby and Mike stood guard so that the couple would not be disturbed as they changed.

Tom and Jenelle quickly helped each other get out of their 'glad rags.' Tom said, "I'd like to start trying to get you preggers right now, but when we get to Monterrey, I look forward to kissing you from head to toe and taking a bath with you. We've got the bridal suite."

Jenelle struck a pose. "Are you sure I can't entice you?"

He laughed. "You're the biggest temptation a man could ever have, and I love you to pieces, but don't you think we should get out of the church first?"

She giggled. "Right you are, my husband! And I love you too!" She threw her arms around him, and they kissed. "So, let's get on the road!"

Less than five minutes later, they were in the car and headed towards the highway.

10.

Tom was half awake, nestled against Jenelle, with one arm draped over her. He kissed her neck.

"Are you awake too?"

"Kind of. This is the latest I've slept in years, but we got to sleep only a couple of hours ago."

"If our skin had not been getting so wrinkled, I think we could have stayed in that whirlpool all night."

Tom chuckled. "I'll get back in there with you any time you're ready."

"Can't we just stay here?" She wiggled against him.

"We can stay in bed all day if you want to, but I heard your stomach growl, and mine has been growling for probably a half-hour or so. How about some breakfast right here in our room?"

"You sound delicious!" She giggled.

"That's not what I meant, but it's a good idea." He tickled her.

"Eeek! I'll get you for that!" She turned to face him and began tickling him."

"Whoa, girl!" He laughed, and then she started laughing uncontrollably. They both turned over onto their backs. In the corner of his eye, he saw a flashing red light. "There's a message for us." He picked up the receiver and pushed zero. "Operator, is there a message for us? Okay." He listened for about thirty seconds, then he hung up. He stretched and yawned.

"Who was the message from?"

"Ruth Branch."

"Our librarian?"

"Yeah. She left a message so as not to disturb us. She has some archeologist friends who want to meet us at the Monterrey Aquarium today, where they are making a presentation. If we go to meet them, they will buy us lunch. So we have a decision. Do we go back to bed after breakfast, or do we go to the aquarium?"

Jenelle stretched and sat up, smiling. "Staying here is a huge temptation, but I've never been to that aquarium. I understand it's got the world's largest aquarium window."

"Shall we make it today's outing?"

"Sure, but let's have breakfast first. Steak and eggs, medium rare, over easy, and all the fixin's, plus Earl Grey if they have it."

"That's good for me, too. Why don't you phone in the order while I make a pit stop?" He got out of bed and headed to the bathroom.

When Tom came out, Jenelle was sitting up in bed, with her hair draped over her chest. "Shall we get some exercise before breakfast?"

Tom grinned. "Absolutely, lover!"

+ + +

The Monterrey Bay Aquarium is situated in old Cannery Row on the ocean. When they got there, the lectures were almost over. As the crowd broke up, Tom and Jenelle went forward and introduced themselves.

"Hello, I'm Tom Kuster, and this is my bride, Jenelle."

"Hello, we're the Cuchins. I'm Leonard, and this is Dava. Congratulations! We understand you're on your honeymoon."

Jenelle nodded. "Yes. We got married yesterday at the conclusion of a worship service in Towne. Ruth Branch left us a message last night to come and see you."

Dava laughed. "I've known Ruth most of my life. She didn't tell us much. She only said that you had given her some rare books to examine, and that we might be interested in what you two have to say."

Tom nodded. "She is quite correct. May we talk about it over lunch?"

Dava smiled. "Certainly, but this is not a good place. Are you familiar with the Pacific Grove area, just south of here?"

Tom nodded. "Yes! I've been there for the Butterfly Days, and I went to a conference at Asilomar."

Dava nodded. "Good. There's a restaurant there called Fandango."

"Yes!" exclaimed Jenelle. "The saffron rice is excellent! They've got some wonderful seafood entrees. Everything is good there."

Leonard nodded. "Good. We'll meet you there in about twenty minutes. We've a reservation in our name."

They made there way out of the aquarium, and it was an easy drive to Fandango. Tom skirted the waterfront so they could see more of the ocean. Their table at Fandango was in a corner surrounded by colorful plants. After they got their water and placed their orders, Tom and Jenelle told of their discovery.

When they paused, Dava put down her fork. "I have never dreamed that there would be another mission, have you, Leonard?"

"No. Now that you've described your find, we'd like to see it. How much more is there to the mission that you've not told us about?"

Jenelle raised her eyebrows. "We don't know. At this point, we're looking for professionals to take the lead and see what is there."

Dava nodded. "Excellent. It will take us a few weeks to raise some money to finance what we call a dig."

Tom shook his head. "That may not be necessary. How much money does it cost for a dig involving just you two for a month or so?"

Leonard grinned. "I'll tell you what. We could set aside the month of July to explore the possibilities. If you'll cover our lodging plus, say, $2,000, we can live with that, can't we, Dava?"

She nodded. "We can easily live on a shoestring for a month." What do you say?"

Tom nodded. "We'll plan on your arrival for the first of July. When you start your work, it will bring the media in, so I'll need to plan ahead for some security."

"Understood."

When they finished their lunch, Leonard and Dava went back to the aquarium, but as Tom and Jenelle got into their car, he said, "It's too cool for us to lie on the beach. What would you like to do?"

Jenelle grinned. "Our hotel has a pool, and we have our swim suits – or at least I've got a bikini. What about you?"

Tom smiled. "I've got a suit."

"Good! Let's just relax by the pool."

"Sounds good!"

Tom started the engine, and as he turned east on Lighthouse Avenue, he glanced at her. "Mom and Dad said they knew we would be getting married when they saw us kissing on the porch at Easter. When in that keen mind of yours did you begin to think in those terms?"

She thought for a moment before answering. "When I kissed you on the cheek by the swimming hole, it was spontaneous, and that moment was on my mind until I went to bed that night. Kissing you that day brought images of kissing Mike. I realized that I was in love with you. What about you?"

"When we kissed on the porch, all I could think about was spending the rest of my life with you. It took me a few hours to sort out why I felt that way, and then as I prayed about it that evening, I remembered the ring."

She looked over at him. "I kind of wondered about that." She paused. "I like Leonard and Dava, don't you?"

"Yeah. I'm going to be really interested in what they find as they explore the rest of our little mission."

"*Our* little mission?"

He grinned. "Well, it *is* on our property."

"True. I want to go back to the aquarium tomorrow morning."

"Whatever you want. Maybe in the afternoon we can go whale watching."

"Yes! Even if we don't see any whales, there're sea otters in the bay. I love watching them." She paused. "I'm thinking ahead about dinner. When Dava and I went to the ladies' room, she told me about a steak house not far from here. She and Leonard had steak and crab, and their steaks were of aged beef so tender they could almost cut them without a knife."

Tom turned into the hotel driveway. "I'm full right now from that rack of lamb and saffron rice. If we don't go this evening, we can go tomorrow."

"Uh huh. That rice was amazing. Did you know that saffron is the world's most expensive spice?"

They got out of the car, and Tom gave the keys to the valet. They walked across the lobby, and then through the open doors of an elevator. Tom touched the button for their floor, and as they closed he asked, "Just for curiosity, how much does saffron cost?"

"I looked it up at the library once. Currently, good-quality saffron runs over $12,000 a pound."

Tom whistled. "Really! That's almost like gold!"

"Right. By comparison, bulk cinnamon is less than $10 a pound. Dava said she thought the saffron we had today was probably from Greece, but most is imported from Iran."

They relaxed by the pool the rest of the afternoon. Tuesday went by all too quickly for both. They did see a whale just a few yards away from their boat, and the steak and crab were memorable.

After eating breakfast on Wednesday in Pebble Beach, at a table overlooking an ocean cliff, they did some sight-seeing before heading back to Towne. Closer to home, as they left the Central Valley, Tom said, "We haven't talked about finances, and I suppose we should."

Jenelle nodded. "Yes. I don't really know how much we'll get for the house that Mike and I owned. My realtor friend, Joan Craver, tells me that the market is a bit unpredictable right now. Why don't we pull into that rest stop up ahead? Nature is calling."

Tom took the off-ramp and pulled into a parking space. "Let's grab a couple of Pepsi's, and we can sit here at one of the picnic tables after we use the restrooms."

"Okay."

Afterward, when they sat down at a picnic table with their drinks, Tom was thoughtful. "I understand how the real estate market is unpredictable right now. Maria and I got several million from the state for the land they took for the highway."

"Really! My house is kind of small – it has just two bedrooms, but it also has that nice den where we used to play cards once in a while.""

"Right. Maria and I split a double tithe of the gross and donated it to several churches and church agencies as anonymous donors. We set aside some of the money for education IRAs for the children, but those were rolled over after the disaster. I've told Juan Smith, our investment counselor, to set you up with a portfolio of your own in addition to mine. He's coming to Towne next week to talk with us. By the way, I've opened a joint checking account at All American Bank. You need to sign a signature card for it."

Jenelle nodded. "I can go in to sign the signature card tomorrow, but you don't need to split the portfolio."

"Are you sure? I was going to suggest we divide the portfolio of stocks, bonds, and funds equally."

She paused. "This is almost overwhelming! "We're millionaires now?"

"Well, we were already millionaires with our land before the money came from the state with our property. Most of our land includes steep hills covered with both apple trees and timber. As you know, the apples are a charity project that Maria and I started. We've been approached for our timber, but I don't want to sell it yet."

"How much land do we have?"

"Just over twenty-one hundred acres are left now, after the highway expansion took about sixty."

"Whoa! I didn't realize we had that much!"

"That's understandable. Mom and Dad acquired it just after World War II when the National Forest Service made the land available pretty cheap. When my parents retired and deeded the land to Maria and I, it only took a short time to pay off the mortgage that my parents had taken out years ago. We got more than we expected from the sale to the state because our lawyer argued successfully that the land had significantly increased in value during the last decade."

Jenelle was thoughtful. "When you mentioned the children and the disaster, it made me think of something we should already have discussed."

"What's that?"

"Mike didn't want to have children. You may remember our telling you and Maria about that a couple of years ago."

Tom nodded. "I remember."

"After the disaster, I stopped taking the pill. I should have discussed it with you, but we've been so busy I didn't even think about birth control. I could already be pregnant. I hope that's okay. It's definitely all right with me."

Tom grinned. You know how much I love kids! I was going to ask you if you wanted to have any with me. I have to say that these last few days it's been fabulous with trying to make you preggers."

She giggled. "Me too!" She finished her drink. "Why don't I drive from here and give you a break?"

"Okay."

The remainder of their drive was uneventful. As they turned off to drive through town, there were lots of cars in the Bill's parking lot. There were a few cars around the Little Red Hen and around the library, but the rest of Towne was quiet.

At Eighth Street, she turned left two blocks, and then she stopped in front of her old house. There was a 'For Sale' sign posted on the lawn. Jenelle put the transmission in park, but she left the engine running. "Mike and I made a lot of memories in that house, but Tom, you and I are now making some wonderful memories of our own."

He nodded. "That's for sure." He paused. "It looks like someone mowed your lawn in the last couple of days."

"Yes. I'll have to thank Joan for that. She was complimentary about how well Mike kept up the place. She said that when I find the right buyer, it will sell easily." Jenelle put the car in drive, and they started off again. "Do you want to stop for something to eat, or would you rather we just eat snacks from the fridge?"

"Let's get home. I'll start a fire in the fireplace if you'll get out some food. I'm sure Mom left us plenty to eat."

Jenelle quickly drove the remaining half-mile to their house. They got their bags out of the car, unlocked the back door, and they went in. When Tom flipped the light switch on, they dropped their bags on the floor. There in the mud room, there was a banner reading, 'Welcome Home!' over the kitchen door."

Taking off and hanging their jackets, they put their shoes on the rack. Jenelle got out her key and unlocked the door. She flipped on the kitchen light. "Tom, come look!"

The kitchen was spotless, and there was a bowl of fresh fruit on the counter. Jenelle saw that there was a note on the fridge, but she did not stop to read it. Instead, she went on into the living room and turned on a lamp. "Wow, Tom! Your Mom and Dad outdid themselves. On a table near the front room bay window was a large vase of flowers. Wood for a fire was already set in the fireplace. Jenelle's furniture was arranged in the midst of Tom's. She smiled. "I like it! I told the movers to leave my sofa with the homeless shelter. This works out fine. What do you think?"

He nodded. "So long as you're happy with this arrangement, I'm happy. If we change our minds, we can rearrange things later. Let's go look at the master bedroom."

As they went in, they saw her dresser next to his, and as she approached the bed, she turned and looked at the closet. "Is that closet door new?"

"Yes. You've a little surprise waiting for you."

As Jenelle opened the closet door, the light came on for a large walk-in closet. "Wow! When did you do this?" As she stepped into the closet, the light came on, and she looked all around. "Terrific, Tom!"

"I finished it a couple of weeks ago. Maria always complained about our not having enough closet space, and the bathroom was small too."

"What do you mean by 'was?'" She opened a door, and there was a bath suite. "You did this too?"

Tom nodded. "I had a lot of help with the plumbing and electrical. I got rid of the utility room by knocking down a wall. It used to have the water heater and a bunch of shelving. There's a tank-less heater in the basement now."

Jenelle threw her arms around him. "I love it! I love you so much!" Leaving the closet, she went to her dresser and opened a drawer. "I owe your Mom a big favor!" She looked in a couple of other drawers. "She saw to it that all my clothes are in the same drawers as before, and clothing in the closet seems to be arranged mostly in the same order as it was at the other house. Fantastic!"

Tom grinned. "After I light the fire in the fireplace, I'll take our luggage, and put all our honeymoon clothing in the laundry room – while you fix us some snacks. Then we can relax and eat." He put his arms around her and gave her a short kiss. "See ya back here in a few minutes."

"I'll be waiting......"

11.

When Tom and Jenelle walked into the station Thursday morning, the phone was ringing. As Tom went on into his office, Jenelle picked up the phone at her desk. "Towne Police Department."

"Hey, Jenelle, this is Will Goodyear."

"Good morning, Will. What's on your mind?"

"I'd like to take Tom to breakfast this morning."

"Hang on, Will." She put her hand over the mouthpiece. "Will wants to buy you breakfast!"

"Okay. Ask him if 7:00 o'clock at the Hen is okay."

"Will, is 7:00 at the Hen okay?"

"Sure. Blessings, Jenelle."

"Bye." She walked into Tom's office and went to the tea brewer. As she filled the basket and started it, she looked over at Tom. "As much as we had to scramble to be here at 6:00, how about we set the alarm for thirty minutes earlier?"

Tom looked up from reading the files stacked on his desk. "I'm thinking an hour earlier so we have time to pray for each other and maybe have devotions."

Jenelle picked up her mug, walked over, and put her hand on his muscular shoulder. "To me, that means we'll have to make time to play during the day, right?"

Tom looked up at her and grinned. "Right!" He pulled her down onto his lap and kissed her."

"Careful! If I spill my tea on your lap, it won't be good!"

Tom let her go. As she got off his lap, he muttered, "The trouble with taking time off is that we have to catch up when we get back," he looked up, "but it sure was worth it."

"You've got that right!" She swung her hips a little extra as she left his office.

Tom was almost through reading all his paperwork when it was time to go to breakfast. As he went past Jenelle's desk he asked, "Shall I bring something back for you?"

She thought a minute. "Ask Effie to make me a breakfast wrap. That'll hold me until lunch."

Tom winked at her. "Okay." In a moment, he was out the door. It was a brisk three-minute walk to the Hen. Inside, he spotted the back of Will's head, and he went and sat down. "Good morning, Will."

"Hey, Tom. Congratulations! You and Jenelle had kind of a short honeymoon. Where'd you go?"

"We went to Monterrey, and we got back last night."

Effie walked up. "Hey, Tom, did you and Jenelle get back last night?" She put a cup of Earl Grey in front of him."

"Good morning, Effie. Thanks. Yeah, we got back last night. I'll have eggs over easy, potatoes, and bacon, no toast. Before I go, I'll have a breakfast wrap to take to Jenelle. That's it."

"Okay. Will, I know what you want, right?"

"Right. Tell the cook, I'll be doing a fire inspection after the noon rush is over."

"Will do. I'll have your food in a minute or two." She walked off.

Will looked at Tom. "I doubt I'll find any problems here at the Hen. They keep this place in good shape. Bill's reopened last night."

"Reopened?"

"Yeah. They were closed Monday and Tuesday. Their rear fire door had to be replaced, and they had let dust accumulate in a couple of places creating a fire hazard. When I saw their grease trap overflowing I did a thorough inspection of that whole place. Those were the worst things. I went back yesterday morning, and Bill had fixed the critical stuff, but I'm going back later this morning. If he doesn't have everything ship shape, he just might be closed this weekend. Mike used to hit him with citations once or twice a year. This was the worst I'd ever seen it and told him so."

Tom nodded. "It sounds like it was pretty bad. I saw where Charly went out there last Saturday to break up a brawl."

"Yeah. Susie and I were there for steaks when it started. I got on my radio and called dispatch while Judy did her best to stop it. Charly arrived a couple of minutes later. I'm sure you know how good he is. Charly had two guys in cuffs and in the back of his patrol car in less than five minutes. Susie and I stood nearby as he took statements. I spotted a pool of water and a shotgun behind the bar. The water was a safety hazard, and that raised a red flag for me. I went back to do a cursory inspection Sunday afternoon, and I found a bunch of other problems, so I shut Bill down."

Tom nodded. Effie came with their food, and they thanked her. He picked up the shakers to put salt and pepper on his eggs. "I'll check out Bill's file when I get back to the office." He took a sip of tea. "While I'm thinking about it, I was in the library a couple of weeks ago, and I noticed that there are no sprinklers in Ruth's work room. She was pushing the room's electrical capacity with a power strip. I told her to talk to Mayor Thompson about putting in another circuit, and the sprinklers that were approved last year should be installed."

"I'll check it out next month when I do the annual inspection, and maybe I'll drop by informally in the next few days." They ate in silence for a while. Will put his fork down and took a swallow of coffee. "I went by Jenelle & Mike's old house on Tuesday. I saw the 'For

Sale' sign. My son is looking for a house. He and my daughter-in-law are looking for a place. It's in good shape, isn't it?"

"Yeah, Mike kept it up real well. It's got three bedrooms, and the layout's pretty good. The grape stake fence around the back yard is only a couple of years old."

"That's good. They've got a big golden retriever that needs to be able to run, and that yard's pretty good size."

Tom nodded. "The realtor's name is Joan Craver, an old friend of Jenelle's." He paused to put his napkin on the table. "Thanks for breakfast, Will. "I've got to get back to the station."

"You're welcome! Let's get together again next week."

Tom nodded. "Okay. See you later." He picked up the breakfast wrap at the kitchen door from Effie, and then he walked briskly back to the station. As he went in the station door, Jenelle looked up as he greeted her. "Hey, beautiful! Anything cookin'?"

"Nope. I'm glad things are quiet. There's lots of stuff to catch up on. Ruth Branch called. After quizzing me about our honeymoon, she asked when you were going to show her the old books in our basement. What old books?"

Tom laughed as he handed her the breakfast wrap. "When I took those books from the mission to Ruth, I didn't tell her where I got them. I previously told her about some books with water damage from a leaking roof that, as a teenager, I had boxed up and put in our basement. I suggested to her that some of them might be pretty old, and that she might like to see them sometime this summer."

Jenelle smiled. "So you didn't lie to her, you just diverted her attention to something else."

"Right. Ruth's always helping teens find odd jobs to do when they're out for the summer. Why don't you talk to her in a few days about getting some teens to work in our basement? With some supervision, they could help clean it out, dry it out, and water-seal it. If you want to, maybe we could put in a spiral stairway instead of that old creaky one we've got."

Jenelle raised her eyebrows. "Finishing off the basement would give us an area of expansion."

"Are you thinking of anything specific?"

She paused, thinking. "Have you ever wanted to have a home theater?"

Tom beamed. "That's a great idea! I wouldn't have the teens install the home theater though...."

"What are you thinking?"

"With the size of property we have, we could begin something with this."

"What?"

The station door opened, and Judy, the waitress from Bill's, walked in. "Hi, you two! Congratulations!"

"Thanks!" they said together.

"Last weekend, Jenelle, I had my hands full with a couple of guys. I've got a couple of bruises to show for my efforts. Can I get together with you soon? I want to brush up on some on my defense skills."

Jenelle nodded. "Sure, Judy." She looked at her husband. "If you can spare me for an hour or so, I'll go with Judy over to the high school. If the gymnastics area is free, we can work there, or there are other possibilities over there."

Tom nodded. "Sure, that's fine."

Judy looked at him. "Before we go, Chief, Bill asked me to check with you on something. He said he's pretty sure that the Fire Chief noticed his shotgun behind the bar. He asked me to check with you on his gun permits." She reached into a back pocket and brought out an envelope. "He said to show you this."

Tom opened the envelope and took out the contents. He looked quickly at each document, and then he went back through and looked more carefully. "Judy, I'll call him. Leave it to me. You can hold on to this and give it back to him when you see him."

"Okay. Is everything in order?"

"Like I said, I'll call him. You go ahead and do your workout with Jenelle."

"Thanks, Chief."

Jenelle got up from her desk and put on her cap and utility belt. On her tiptoes, she gave Tom a peck on the cheek, and then the two women were out the door.

Tom smiled and scratched his head, and then he went back to his desk in his office. Sitting down, he punched a familiar number for his small community. "Bill? This is Chief Kuster."

"Hey, Chief. Did Judy give you that envelope?"

"Yeah, I looked it over and gave it back to her. I was surprised."

"Surprised?"

"This is not like you, Bill. Up until now, you've been pretty good about keeping all your permits up to date."

"Yeah. Sorry, Chief."

"We've known each other a long time, Bill. We can either keep this simple or get the district attorney involved."

"How do we keep it simple?"

"We can do it all through Judge Clemmens. You saw him yesterday, just like every month, for Pumas' Club. Call him and tell him I said you've screwed up. He may be willing to do it all in chambers. You need to do this today, Bill."

"Am I going to jail?"

"I hope not. That's up to Judge Clemmens. Talk to him today, Bill."

"Okay."

"See ya later." Tom hung up and dialed another number. "Toby, this is Tom Kuster."

"Good morning, Tom. Did you have a nice honeymoon?"

"Monterrey was terrific, and you know Jenelle."

The district attorney chuckled. "That I do, Tom. What's up with you this morning?"

"I just got off the phone with Bill Jacobs. He's screwed up, and I told him so. Last weekend, Will spotted a shotgun behind the bar. He told me about it this morning. He sent Judy over here to the station with an envelope full of outdated and incomplete paperwork. You and I have both known Bill for years. He's a generally decent businessman, but what I saw was not good. I told him to call the judge today and talk with him. I also told him that the judge might be able to deal with it in chambers. I did not tell Bill that I was calling you, or that you have to get involved. He asked me if he was going to jail, and I told him that I hoped not."

"Do you want a warrant to search Bill's place? He lives upstairs on the premises."

Tom scratched his head. "To do this right, I think a search has to be executed. If you can get a warrant this afternoon, I'll send Jack over to execute it with you, Toby. You've got a pretty good investigator as I recall."

"Yeah, she's very good, and she likes Jack too."

"Really? I've never tried to be a matchmaker."

Toby laughed. "Even if you or I tried, Dannie is her own woman. I'll get that warrant right now and call Jack at home."

"Good. Talk to you later, Toby." Tom hung up. The rest of the day seemed unusually busy with small stuff for both Tom and Jenelle.

+ + +

Friday morning, while Tom went to the County Courthouse and sat down with Judge Clemmens, Jenelle went to the Little Red Hen to get some breakfast before going to the station. Walking in, she smelled bacon cooking, when her eyes grew wide. Sitting in a booth were Leonard and Dava Cuchins, and they were waving at her. She waved back and walked over. "This is a pleasant surprise! I wasn't expecting to see you until next month!"

Dava smiled. "We know. Will you join us for breakfast?"

"Sure, but I won't be able to chat very long. I have to be at the station in about thirty minutes, and Tom's over at the Courthouse."

Leonard nodded. "We know we should have called, but we're headed south for a consultation near Santa Barbara, and we're just passing through."

Dava smiled and lowered her voice. "Yes. We spent last night at a motel across from a bar and grill, and we can spend another night there if we can take a quick look at your find." She looked up as Effie was approaching.

Effie smiled at Jenelle. "They've already ordered. What would you like?"

"I've not a lot of time, so I'll have Earl Grey, toast with preserves, and three strips of bacon."

"Coming right up." Effie walked away.

His voice lower, Leonard asked, "Is there any way we can spend thirty minutes or so taking a cursory look at your dig?"

Jenelle took out her cell phone, pressed a button, and put it to her ear. "Hey, handsome, I'm here in the Hen with a surprise. I'm sitting here having breakfast with the Cuchins." She listened. "Right. They just want to take a preliminary look." She listened. "Okay. See you in about thirty." She put away her phone. "Tom is going to ask one of the other deputies to cover for us at the station while we give you a quick tour."

Dava was delighted. "That's terrific!" She lowered her voice. "We'll talk more about this when we get there."

Effie came with their food, and Jenelle chatted with them about the community and its features as they ate.

A little over a half-hour later, Jenelle, Tom, and the Cuchins drove up to the swimming hole, and Tom parked near the generator. As they got out, Leonard asked, who owns this land?"

"We do." Jenelle smiled. "As soon as Tom gets the generator going, we'll take you to the cave. I'm glad you both have shoes suitable for this area."

Dava laughed. "We hardly ever wear dress shoes except to formal lectures or church." A hum started nearby. "Is that the generator? It's really quiet."

Tom walked up. "Yes. I didn't want the generator to disturb anyone using the lake at night."

Jenelle took Dava's hand. "Come on, Dava, we'll make it ladies first."

When they got to the boulders, Dava asked, "Where's the cave?"

Tom reached under a rock's edge. "Right here." He swung the fake boulder out of the way.

Leonard grinned. "That's ingenious!"

Tom nodded. "It was Jenelle's idea. I'll go first. Jenelle will close the door behind us."

Once inside, Leonard and Dava stared in all directions. "It's more than merely pretty, Jenelle. It's actually quite beautiful, isn't it Leonard?" Dava asked.

"Indeed! Looking at the hillside, you would not think a cave this large would lie within."

"Tom and I figured out that the ceiling is probably not more than ten feet thick. A long time ago, a slab of rock slid down the hill to cover the opening." Jenelle pointed. "Come over this way."

Tom let Jenelle lead the way. "My deceased son, Tommie, found this cave one day. My first wife and daughters were killed with Tommie and never saw it."

Jenelle took the night stick flashlight and pointed at the door jamb. "If you look carefully, you'll see that this all is man-made."

Leonard used his flashlight to examine the entire perimeter of the doorway. "I've seen doorways like this in many Native American homes."

Tom stepped up. "Now I'll turn on the portable floodlight. It will make things easier." He turned it on, and carried it into the chapel.

"My! I see why you've drawn the preliminary conclusions that you have!" Dava was enthusiastic.

"Yes," Leonard exclaimed. "Tom, can you bring your floodlight closer to the cot?" As Tom did so, Leonard examined the bier. "Yes! This is definitely a monk's alb." He touched the blanket midway down the bulge on the cot. "Dava! We'll have to treat this with great care, but not now. I think there's a cross under the blanket here. Wonderful!" Leonard stood up straight.

Dava pointed, "What's through there?"

Jenelle moved. "Come and look. We'll need the flood, Tom." They moved through the next doorway and stopped just short of the pool. "We tested this water, and it's like the spring water that feeds the lake down the hill."

Tom pointed. "Come over here." He led them to the stairs. "These are not rock but masonry. Jenelle tried to go up carefully, but the third stair gave way."

Leonard nodded. "Yes, I see. Tom, point that flood up the stairs more directly." They all tried to see what was beyond the landing at the top. "I think we'll have to lay a ladder on top of the steps in order to get up there."

Dava looked carefully the area at the bottom of the stairs. "Yes. A ladder will suffice. We'll simply have to anchor it to the rock in some way. Come, Leonard, we don't have time for more today. Let's let Tom and Jenelle get back to work."

They started making their way out. In the main cave, Dava pointed up to the right to the opening. "Is that the vent you told us about?"

Jenelle took off her knapsack and took out the air rifle. "Yes." She put in a shuttlecock and began pumping. "Watch, you'll see. Tom, do you want to try to catch it?"

"Sure! Why not." He stepped back about ten paces. When Jenelle fired, the shuttlecock flew further than he expected, and he almost didn't catch it. "Got it! There's a real breeze up there coming from somewhere." He handed the shuttlecock to Jenelle, and she put things back into her knapsack.

Tom led them back to the tunnel and opened the door again. Outside, he sat down on a rock until the other three were all out, and Jenelle closed and latched the rock door. "I'm glad you came today. Do you now have a better idea of what you're looking for?"

Leonard nodded. "Even with the little we've seen, we can almost be certain that this was a mission of some kind. It occurs to me that perhaps Native Americans occupied the area previously, and when the priests arrived, they simply adapted what was already here. What do you think, Dava?"

"That's entirely possible. I think we'll know more when we see what's on that upper level. I'm glad we came, too. I thought maybe Tom and Jenelle here had exaggerated their find a bit. It would not have been the first time in our careers. Instead, I think there's a lot more here than what's been seen thus far."

Leonard nodded. "I agree, Dava. This could well be a major find. When we come in July, I think it would be best if we don't stay in a motel. We're going to need workspace outside of the cave."

Jenelle looked at her husband. "I've got an idea, Tom. I can delay the availability of my old house until August or even September."

"Are you sure?" Tom raised his eyebrows.

"Absolutely! Leonard, Dava, how would you like to have a house to work in?"

"That would be great! Dava was enthusiastic. "We'll have to rent some basic furniture and a couple of tables to work on. What do you think, Leonard?"

He nodded. "It's a good solution, if you don't mind, Jenelle."

"Not a bit. Let's go back down the hill."

By the car, Tom pointed at the dam. "That dam has some severe problems. The contractor I've hired is going to put a large gated aqueduct section behind the dam, put earth berms either side, and then remove the dam. He's also going to do some non-explosive demolition around the cave's tunnel and install a similar tunnel of steel-re-enforced concrete. An electrician is going to put more circuits to the cave."

Leonard beamed. "Excellent! There's no way of knowing how stable that hillside is, is there?"

Jenelle smiled. "Actually, we had a highly qualified geologist examine the entire area, and she's advising the contractor. It'll all be done before you get here in July."

Dava nodded. "Fantastic! Leonard, let's get back to our motel. We can take a nap before dinner, and then we can get back on the highway early tomorrow."

Leonard shook Tom's hand. "Thank you in advance for this opportunity." He headed for the car, and the others followed.

12.

Sunday morning, Jenelle and Tom did not get up until almost 6:00. Over breakfast, they talked about the visit by the Cutchins. While Tom took an unexpected call from Judge Clemmens, Janelle cleaned up their breakfast dishes and took a quick shower. They ended up heading out the door with time enough to spare to get to the 9:00 AM church service.

As worship was concluding, Pastor Gentle called Tom and Jenelle forward. "When the two of you got married there was no time for a reception. This morning is another matter. In our dining hall, there's a cake waiting to be cut."

It was nearly noon when the party began to wind down. After a swift trip home to put on their uniforms, Jenelle took the patrol car to the station after a quick stop at Ben's for hamburgers and fries. When Tom came in a few minutes later, his eyes lit on the hamburgers. "Ben's?"

"Yep. I didn't eat much of that cake. It was too much sweet too early in the day."

Tom kissed her on the cheek. "You've got that right. This looks just right until this evening."

Jenelle swallowed. "While waiting for the fries, I was thinking about that ribs place twelve miles down the highway for dinner."

"That sounds good except both Jack and Charly are off this evening. We've got to cover. Charly goes off duty at five. That really sounds good though." Tom took a big bite of his hamburger.

"We can call in our order, and..." she took a drink from her soda. "...and I can pick it up and take it to the house. I really don't want to cook tonight. We'll be on call from the house, as we often are."

"You know it's not hard to sell me on ribs. Get a couple of full racks, and any leftovers can go in the fridge." He took a bite of his hamburger, and he looked out the window. Everything was quiet, which was typical for a Sunday. "What time does Ruth Branch come over tomorrow?"

Jenelle nodded as she chewed. "I told her to come sometime after 8:00. You'll easily be back from breakfast by then. I'll be going out to my old house to see about getting some basic furnishings for July into it. I told my friend Joan not to show it again until further notice. I also said that it most certainly could be shown again in September."

Tom nodded.

+ + +

Monday morning, Tom was in their garage, getting the truck out and putting the car in, when he saw Ruth pulling into the driveway. He waved and pointed toward the front door as he headed toward the back door. He got through the house and to the front door, just as she knocked. He opened the door. "Good morning Ruth! How are you?"

"I'm fine thanks. It appears both you and Jenelle are happy and healthy."

"That we are. Come this way." Tom led Ruth through the living room and to the hall, where the basement door was on the left. He opened the door and flipped on the light switch. "I'll go first. I think there are no cobwebs, but I'll make sure."

Ruth followed him down. "I think the last time I was in this house, your parents were celebrating their thirty-fifth wedding anniversary."

"That was a while ago. It smells damp down here, but there are no puddles. The books are in these boxes over here." He went to some crude shelving. "Jenelle and I unboxed the books last week and put them on the shelves. They're pretty fragile."

Ruth picked one up. "Oh, My! *Huckleberry Finn*." She turned a page. "It's not a first edition, but it is copyrighted over a hundred years ago. If you'll let me take it back with me to the library, I'll have my archivist friend look at it next week when she looks at the others."

"There are a couple of clean strong boxes," he pointed, "over there. Take any that you want with you back to the library. I've got to go back upstairs because Paul Peterson will be here in a few minutes."

"The contractor?"

Tom nodded. "Jenelle and I want to upgrade and finish off this basement. Dave Moore will be coming in to do some wiring work. I know you like to help high-school students find work in the summer. This will be a good project."

"Hmmm. The labor would be simple enough, wouldn't it?"

"Yeah. Paul will supervise and organize everything but the wiring work, and Dave Moore will supervise the electrical work.

A voice came from the top of the stairs. "Did I hear my name just now?" Dave came down the stairs. "Good morning, Tom. Hi, Ruth." Ruth looked up from a book and nodded while Dave shook Tom's hand."

Tom grinned. "I need your expertise to tell me what can and can't be done. Paul Peterson will be here in a few minutes, so the three of us can put our heads together. Jenelle and I are talking about upgrading the half-bath and putting in partitions for a home theater, a small workshop, and a recreation room."

"Good morning!" Paul Peterson came down the stairs. "You left the door open, Tom, and with Dave's truck here I thought I could come on in."

Tom shook his hand. "Good morning! Yes, that's fine. I left the door open for a reason. I was just going to say to Dave that most people don't realize that this house has a full basement under the entire structure."

Paul craned his head to peer around the stairs, and whistled. "This basement is huge!"

"It's old, too. I've never checked the Towne records to see who built this place. It might be interesting to find out some of the history of this house."

"I've got most of those records at the library," Ruth called out.

Tom nodded. "Thanks, Ruth." He paused. "I'm wanting the two of you to supervise teen labor this summer, to make sure everything is done according to code. It does not have to all be done this summer, of course."

Dave pointed. "There's where the electricity comes into the house, but the main panel is outside."

"Right. We've also got natural gas. Paul, I eventually want to put in a convection floor furnace so that we'll have heat when there's a power failure. We don't want to use the fireplace always during power failures."

Dave nodded his head. "Although it's good to have a floor furnace as a backup in case the HVAC fails, I think that, since you have gas available, you should put a two hundred kilowatt generator on a slab right outside there." He pointed. "It can be wired to come on automatically anytime there's a power failure. I don't know about your budget, though."

Tom grinned. "At this point, Jenelle and I are not worried about the cost. The generator sounds like a good idea, Dave. Let's do it." Tom pointed. "Paul, we have plenty of space, so Jenelle and I want to put a home theater in this area near the foot of the stairs. Then...." he pointed to the other side of the stairs. "We can partition off a large recreation room. I want you to plan it so that, if needed, it can be further partitioned at a future date."

The three men started walking towards the other side of the house. When they came to the bathroom, Paul said, "I didn't even imagine there would be this half bath down here."

Dave flipped on the switch. "Not bad. Just a basin and a toilet. You said earlier you want to upgrade it. What do you have in mind?"

Tom pointed. "Paul, believe it or not, that toilet is the lowest point the sewer goes for the house before dropping down to the sewer. Since the house is on a hill, the main sewer line under the street is nearly seventy feet from here."

Paul nodded. "And you're telling this to me because?"

"Jenelle wants this to be made into a full bath with a tub shower combination. Then, on the right, the other side of the current bathroom wall, we want to know if it's practical to put in a hot tub in a room the size of a small bedroom, with a window through the basement wall to the outside. Outside, right here, the hill falls away rapidly, and the basement floor is only about a foot below the ground outside."

Paul nodded. "I hope I can find some old blueprints at the building department for this house. It will make it easier to get plans and permits done."

"Right." Tom nodded. "Dave, I'm glad you're taking notes. I know next to nothing about electrical circuit requirements."

"I'll take care of it. I've just gotten an idea, and it involves you, Paul, if you're interested."

"What's that?"

"You and I both have kids and like working with kids, right?" Paul nodded, and Dave went on. "Do you know some plumbing, carpentry, drywall, and other contractors nearby who like working with kids?"

Both Tom and Paul began to smile, and as Paul nodded he said, "I think I know where you're going with this, Dave. We can start a trade school, on paper only at first. This would be our first project."

"Yes!" Tom was excited. "That's a great idea! My lawyer, Everett Beam, can do the legal work so that qualified contractors in our area can take on high-school students as apprentice workers. Paul, as a general contractor, you'll have your work cut out for you. It could bring business to the whole area."

The men talked about it the rest of the morning, while they sketched plans for the basement. Ruth Branch got the men to carry boxes of books to her car, so she could take them to the library.

+ + +

Wednesday morning it was very warm, and the sky was clear. Even though the first day of summer was more than a week away, John Simpson knew that it was going to get hot. Tuesday evening, during the last hours of daylight, John had triple checked his measurements before having his men drill the quarry holes above the tunnel entrance. The sun was beginning to set when they the filled the holes with the non-explosive demolition grout. Overnight, the grout had expanded, and this morning he had a crew coming in to remove the debris.

He looked up as he heard, then saw a large flatbed truck making its way through the trees. John signaled his dam crew, and they came to unload the truck. It took them less than thirty minutes to place the larger steel-re-enforced tunnel into the cave above the generator gate. The other one they placed on rented pontoons, so they could float it into position behind the dam. John waved when he saw Tom driving up in his pickup. "Hey, Tom!"

Tom nodded. "I see you're making progress."

"Yeah. I talked to your deputy, Jack, and he'll get here in a couple of hours. No one can get into the cave right now because of the debris that piled up as that part of the hill gave way last night."

"Do you mean the demolition is already done?"

John nodded. "It happened slowly, but surely, overnight last night. Behind those boulders, is a bunch of rocks mixed with vegetative debris. It'll all be gone in a couple of hours, long before lunch. Your deputy will keep an eye on things all day. In the early afternoon, we'll place that square prefab unit," he pointed, "into position. As you can see, it has a built-in security gate. We'll place the larger rocks around it, and then we'll lace the area with rebar. Late this afternoon, if everything stays on schedule, a gunite pump will be here to seal the job. I'm glad the ground is dry now, because the trucks coming in are pretty heavy."

Tom nodded. "I'm impressed, John, but then I knew that you were a pro. What about the dam?"

"We'll be done by Friday, unless there's unforeseen problems. On a hunch, I brought over a crew yesterday, and we re-enforced the old dam with some temporary abutments that should easily hold until the new one is in place. If it breaks while we're putting in the new one, we'll just have to work as fast as we can continuously, until the new one is fixed up. Your Fire Chief, Will Goodyear, has sandbags set aside in case there's flooding, but I don't think that'll happen."

Tom smiled. "Thanks, John. I'll come by this evening to see the cave."

"Okay." John ambled off.

Tom got back into his truck. He started the engine and turned on the air conditioning, but he left it in park. Taking his cell phone, he dialed his most familiar number. "Hey, it's me. Jack's going to be over here all day with the tunnel, which should be secure by the end of the day. The dam will take the rest of the week."

"Have you talked to Dave yet?"

"No, that's my next call. One of us needs to be at the station tomorrow while the other walks Dave through the cave."

"I'll stay here." She sounded firm. "You know more about electrical stuff."

Tom laughed. "Not by much!"

"Maybe. How soon'll you be done there?"

"As soon as I talk to Dave, I'm heading out."

"Ruth Branch called, and she said the archivist suggests you auction off at least some of those books from the basement. I'm thinking that if we do that, we can donate the proceeds to the library."

"Good idea!" Tom was enthusiastic. "The alternative is to let the library have them on long-term loan. We're not going to make any use of them anyway. Tell Ruth to go ahead and make the arrangements she thinks are appropriate."

"Okay. I won't tell her about donating the proceeds though."

"Right. See ya in a little bit. I love you."

"I love you too."

After he hung up, Tom called Dave Moore, arranging to see him the next morning. He put his truck in gear and headed out the back way to the highway. Once on the road, he headed towards the turnoff for Towne. Less than five minutes later, he walked into the station. Jenelle had her back to the door, peering into a file cabinet. "You look almost as nice from the back as from the front!"

"Thank you, kind sir!"

Tom headed into his office, stopping at his corner table to brew a cup of tea. As it brewed, he heard the air-conditioning click on. While pulling out his chair to sit down, Jenelle walked in. He looked up and said, "Things are moving along faster than I expected out by the swimming hole."

She nodded. "I assume you saw John when you got out there. He was there last evening."

"John's a pro. I'm confident the new dam will be secure by Friday afternoon. I just hope we don't lose too much water in the process."

"It'll be fine, but I'm concerned about security on our other project."

"The door is very strong, and the padlock is the best of its kind."

Jenelle nodded again. "I don't doubt that. Still, we're protecting something that's historically priceless. What about having an alarm that sends an alert to our cell phones?"

Tom was thoughtful. "You may be right. Why don't you make a few calls, ...no, ...wait." He paused. "I overheard a conversation at the church in San Francisco last Fall. Call Community Evangelical Church in San Francisco. They had a guest lecturer in his seventies who used to be a career thief and very successful. Now he's embraced Jesus and does lectures on security." Jenelle started to smile as he continued. "Try to get hold of him. He'll be an ideal expert for us."

Jenelle looked up at the ceiling. "Thanks Lord!" She looked back at Tom and grinned. "Who'd of thought we'd be asking advice from this kind of source!" She turned and went back to her desk.

+ + +

Early Friday morning, Jenelle was working on the next month's schedule when the station door opened, and a small, wiry, white-haired man came in, walking with a cane. "Are you Patrolwoman Jenelle Kuster?"

"I am. What can I do for you, sir?"

"I'm Jim Fitzgerald. We talked on the phone on Wednesday about a special security challenge you have."

Jenelle's mouth hung open for a moment. "Yes! I must say I'm more than a little surprised."

The old man grinned. "I don't blame you. When you called, I was at the church to see an old friend. I actually live just 17 miles up the highway here from Towne."

Jenelle cocked her head. "Have I seen you at the Little Red Hen?"

"You probably have. I come in for smoked ham and eggs about once a week. Effie is an old friend. I think I saw you having breakfast with the Fire Chief a time or two."

Jenelle smiled. "That was my first husband. He was killed, along with the Police Chief's family in that train derailment last year."

Jim nodded. "I remember that tragedy." He paused. "I had to come by personally, because I am seldom presented with a security situation that really challenges me. Do you mind if I sit down?"

Jenelle smiled and pointed at a chair. "Please continue." She found herself sizing him up, considering what she knew of the man.

"In my years on the other side of the law, I broke into some of the most secure buildings in the world, usually without detection. In my retirement, I'm able to recommend systems based upon nearly every situation. Yours is not a building, however, and this was a head scratcher."

"Was?"

He nodded. "I've come up with a system with only three parts, though I would recommend making it five, or maybe six."

"Go on." Jenelle was totally focused.

"The first part of the system would be one or more ground movement sensors. They detect any kind of movement or vibration within twenty-five meters, even movement as minuscule as the soil disturbed by a small rodent. The second part of the system is a combination computer and transmitter. It receives the data from such sensors to determine whether data coming in is important or not. If it computes something that it is programmed to detect, it turns on the transmitter, transmits the data with interpretation, and shuts it off again."

Jenelle nodded. "I suppose the third part of the system is on the receiving end."

"Yes. Any monitoring service – or even your own department – can handle that." He reached into a sweater pocket and handed her a thumb drive. "All the information on the equipment is here. Installation by a security specialist is not required. It can be done by a qualified electrician. I've also put detailed instructions on there." He stood up. "I've got enough investments for retirement I don't charge for my services. Besides, I live nearby, and I'm part of the community. Just buy me a cup of tea sometime."

"We've got a tea brewer in the Chief's office, if you'd like a cup of Earl Grey or English Breakfast."

"Thank you! That would be enjoyable. Do you have decaf by any chance?"

"Sure! What'll it be?"

"Decaf Earl Grey, if you please."

The station door opened, and Tom walked in. "Hello, sir. Are you being helped?"

"Yes, thank you. I'm Jim Fitzgerald."

"The security man?" Tom extended his hand.

"Yes." They shook hands.

Jenelle returned with two mugs of tea and handed one to him. "I didn't ask if you wanted sugar."

Jim shook his head. "None, but thank you." He took a sip and smiled. "You did not use a tea bag, did you. This is bulk tea?" he asked.

"Yes. We have a single-cup coffee brewer that never sees coffee. It has a stainless steel cup for the tea leaves. It was a gift to us, or rather, to the Chief."

Tom was curious. "Your visit is unexpected."

"Yes. I've given your deputy a thumb drive with my recommendations and instructions. I do hope that some day I'll be able to see your discovery after the archeologists are done."

Tom nodded. "That can be arranged. My deputy here," he put his arm around her, "is also my wife." He looked at Jenelle. "The dam is finished, and John and his crew will be gone in less than an hour."

"Already? That's great!"

Jim looked at them. "A dam?"

Jenelle nodded. "The town swimming hole is up near the archeological dig. J & J construction has both secured the cave and created a new dam this week."

13.

Leonard and Dava Cuchins arrived on the thirtieth of June, and they moved into Jenelle's old house. Jenelle gave them keys to both the house and the cave. They were also given the phone number of the security monitoring service, so that the service could be notified each instance there was someone going into the cave.

Dave Moore installed lighting in the main cave with outlets. Leonard and Dava could use extension corded lighting for the entire cave complex.

At 6:00 AM on July third, Jenelle was at the station, while Tom was sitting in the Hen having breakfast with the Fire Chief. Will was relaxed as he explained how he prepared for the celebration to take place the next night. "I've got my fishing boat tied up at the picnic area. I've got a raft loaded with fireworks anchored fifty yards above the dam and a good distance from the picnic area. I've got a rotation of firemen keeping an eye on everything until we set off the show tomorrow night."

Tom sipped his Earl Grey and nodded. "I know you're well prepared for this, Will. I'll be glad to pay your men for their time."

Will shook his head. "That won't be necessary. All the guys volunteered because they want a good show for their families. Just before nine o'clock, a couple of them will go to the raft to the middle and set things off on the hour. I'll have our pumper standing by in case there are any problems, and there are a couple of other community pumpers that will be standing by near the highway."

"Good. I was going to supply about the same amount of fireworks as the last few years, but Jenelle wanted a bigger show this year because we're going to be making some announcements. She alerted Barbara, the reporter at the courthouse."

Will nodded. "Tomorrow should be a memorable Fourth of July. I've got things I've gotta be doing. Thanks for the breakfast."

Tom smiled. "You're welcome. I'll be seeing you tomorrow." They both got up, and Tom put the bill on his tab.

A few minutes later, as Tom walked in the station door, Jenelle was on the phone. "No, Ruth, since we're loaning those books to the library on indefinite loan, we're leaving it to you as to how they are displayed." She smiled. "You're welcome, Ruth. I'll see you tomorrow evening. Bye." She looked up. "Hi, handsome! Ruth's bringing eight teens to the house on the fifth to start their apprenticeships. The unions are on board for the apprenticeships because the Mayor made some calls."

Tom smiled. "Excellent! Have you heard from the Cuchins?"

She nodded. "Dava's been in touch with Community College, and four or five students are going to help them for two to three weeks starting next Monday. Dava crawled up a ladder that she and Leonard put on the stairs. There may have been a small tribe living there before the Franciscans got there."

Tom nodded, raising his eyebrows. "Interesting!"

"There's one more thing." She got up, went around her desk, and put her arms around his neck. "I'm seeing Dr. Beebee the day-after tomorrow. I think I'm pregnant." She grinned.

Tom beamed. "Wow! That's terrific!"

She kissed him and smiled. "This does not mean we should stop trying, you know."

Tom chuckled as he nodded. "I think we should keep up the effort, don't you?"

Jenelle nodded and smiled. "No argument here!"

+ + +

The Fourth of July began warm and got hot. By 3:00 in the afternoon, the temperature had climbed past a hundred, and the Towne Fire Department got two calls to put out small brush fires along the highway.

As with previous years, picnickers began gathering at the lake in the early afternoon. Brad Williams, The fireman whom Jenelle hadn't seen since Mike was killed, was there to watch the portable grills that had been set up by various families, including his own. A commercial refrigerator that Tom had rented for the day was quietly humming near the generator. Beside it was a rented freezer containing several hundred pounds of crushed ice.

The lights under the lake came on at dusk, though at first no one noticed. All the police and fire personnel were there, and all were at least theoretically on duty. About 8:30, Jenelle went to the portable lectern and loudspeaker and turned it on. Mayor Thompson stepped up to the mike. "Good evening, everyone! For those who don't know me, I'm Jules Thompson, Mayor of Towne. On behalf of all of us, I'd like to begin by thanking Tom and Jenelle Kuster, not only because all this is their property, and because they're provided generously for our July Fourth party, but because they've lit the lake this year. It's beautiful." There was applause and a few cheers. The fireworks are at 9:00, but Tom and Jenelle have announcements to make. Tom?"

Tom stepped up to the mike. "We have some mixed feelings tonight because, as probably all of you know, last fall, there was a train derailment, and my family and Jenelle's first husband were killed. As we look at all of you, we remember all the times when you enjoyed this day with Mike Robbins setting off the fireworks, and my first wife Maria making sure that everyone had what they needed. It seemed like my three kids, Tommie, Alice, and Karen, were in the water all day." There were murmurs of agreement. "This year, Mike, Maria, Tommie, Alice, and Karen are watching this from heaven."

As Tom stopped to wipe his eyes, Jenelle came to the mike. "Tom and I started leaning on each other, and it seemed very natural when we fell in love and got married." There was scattered applause. "We will not know for sure until tomorrow when I see the doctor, but I think I'm pregnant." She stepped away from the mike when there was applause.

Tom kissed her forehead. "Now, I'd like to introduce some guests we have here tonight. Tom and Dava, will you wave at everybody?" They waved. "Tom and Dava Cuchins are archaeologists, and they are here because of something my deceased son Tommie discovered. Up the hill from here, behind the generator a ways, is a cave that Tommie discovered. When Mike and I went into it the first time to check it out, we detected methane gas, so we sealed it off for safety reasons."

There was murmuring in the crowd, and Jenelle came back to the mike. "My first husband had the air tested, and the quantity of methane was very small, and deep into the cave. A few weeks after the disaster, Tom decided to tell me about a secret that he and Mike had shared. Tom had given a few books to Ruth Branch, Towne's librarian, not telling her where they came from. Tonight, Ruth," she nodded at her, "we're telling you that those books came from the cave."

"Really???!!!!" Ruth almost shouted.

Tom put his arm around Jenelle as he got closer to the mike. "The archaeologists, Leonard and Dava Cuchins, are here because the cave is actually an undocumented mission of Francisco Palóu and Junípero Serra." There was murmuring in their audience. "One of the books is a journal of Francisco Palóu. Jenelle and I are providing the books on more or less permanent loan to the Towne library. You can ask Ruth Branch as to how soon they will be on display." Tom nodded to her.

Jenelle squeezed closer to the mike. "For much of the summer, you will be seeing the Cuchins and a few students from Towne Community College, who will be scientifically examining the cave. They hope to have some results for us and for the public before the end of the summer." There was scattered applause. "Please do not try to enter the cave unless you have permission. The archeologists have lots of work to do, and they need everyone not on their crew to stay away until they have completed their work."

Tom looked at his watch. "Now, when I turn off the underwater lights, that's the signal to our Fire Department to start the show." As Jenelle turned off the amplifier in the podium, Tom went to the generator shed and turned off the lights. The show was spectacular.

The next morning, both Tom and Jenelle were at the station after a stop at the Hen for breakfast. Tom was reading an accumulation of mail when the phone rang, and Jenelle answered. "Towne Police Station."

"Good morning, Jenelle. This is Paul. How are you and Tom today?"

"We're fine, Paul. What's up with you?"

"Well, now that your basement is dry, the kids are going to learn how to do dry walling. It's hard work, and I'm thinking ahead to your home theater installation. Have you and Tom decided definitely on a projector and screen?"

"Just a moment, I'll get Tom on the line with us." She called out, "Tom, can you pick up on this call with me, and with Paul?"

Tom picked up the phone. "What's up, Paul?"

"I just asked Jenelle if you two had definitely decided on a projector and screen."

"We've been discussing the pros and cons of projection versus a big flat screen."

Jenelle interjected, "A projection system can be bigger and more like a theater, but with a flat screen we wouldn't have to have the lights out, and...."

Paul interrupted. "I've been talking with an expert in San Jose, and when I told him about all the space available, he suggested a compromise – rear projection."

"How would that work, Paul?" Tom took a swallow of Earl Grey.

"If you do it this way, we establish a small, permanently dark room behind the screen. The screen is kind of like a black-framed window, only instead of glass it's a translucent screen. The projector is mounted below the 'window' and projects on a front-surface mirror on the opposite wall, which reflects the projection onto the back of the translucent window. The front speakers are in the wall either side and below the window. The sub-woofer is also in an enclosure beneath the window. What do you two think?"

Tom nodded at Jenelle through his doorway, and she responded. "It sounds good, Paul."

"Great! I can start the kids on it this afternoon, and your basement will be mostly done before they have to go back to school."

Tom continued to nod. "I'm hanging up now, Paul. I've got some other calls to make. You can tell

Jenelle what happens next." He hung up, and he saw Jenelle nodding at him through the door.

"What's next, Paul?"

"I think that with the apprentice workers from Community College, your basement will be completely finished by the end of September. I'm still waiting for the new spiral staircase, so if it's late that could push us into October. By the way, the high school kids said to tell you that if you'll pay them the same rate, that they'll do the painting on weekends after school starts."

Jenelle laughed. "I'm sure they have the best of intentions, but I would not want their painting the basement to be a substitute for their doing their homework!"

"Right!" He laughed. "We'll talk again tomorrow. Take care."

"Bye." She hung up.

+ + +

On an evening in the middle of August, Tom and Jenelle were putting away the dinner dishes when the doorbell rang. As Tom continued to put dishes and pots away, Jenelle went to the door and saw that it was the Cuchins. She opened the door saying, "Good evening! Come on in!"

Dava smiled. "We hope we're not interrupting dinner."

Jenelle shook her head. "No, we were just cleaning up. Come in and make yourselves comfortable."

Tom walked into the living room. "Good evening." He shook Leonard's hand. "Are you almost finished?"

As they sat down, Leonard handed Tom a large envelope. "That's a summary. In a couple of months, we'll send you our analysis. We've finished exposing and cataloging all the artifacts in the complex. We're not removing anything at this point. In the envelope with the key to the cave is a thumb drive with about twelve hundred high-resolution images. The last page has some recommendations."

Dava nodded. "As you know, your late son's discovery is now public knowledge. You're going to be hearing from the University of California, from at least two different campuses, wanting to have students spend time here. You may also hear from other universities."

Jenelle smiled and nodded. "We've already heard from UCLA."

Leonard nodded. "You'll be getting requests for the next several years at least. Since weather will never be an issue, you'll have to schedule different groups at varied times – that is if you want them doing more research."

Tom nodded. "We're praying about it." We'll email copies of the images you've made to anyone who requests them. What about lighting beyond the main cave?"

Leonard shook his head. "I don't recommend permanent lighting beyond what you've already done. It would be too easy to do further damage to the cave's environment."

"Further damage?"

Dava laughed. "Don't worry! We archeologists like everything to be pristine, untouched by anyone but professionals. You two handled this whole dig very well." She stood up, and Leonard followed. "We have packing to do because we're leaving early tomorrow morning."

Leonard turned back to face them. "We can't thank you enough for the use of your house, Jenelle. It was perfect for our needs. Can we drop off the key at the Police Station on our way out tomorrow?"

"Sure. There'll be someone on duty all day."

"Great! Thanks again." They all shook hands, and Leonard and Dava made their way out.

Closing the door, Jenelle said, "I'm going to miss them."

"Me too." He paused. "Now that the new staircase is installed, let's go downstairs. Paul is coming tomorrow morning at eight to the station. He says that since we're almost done, he wants to talk about something else for our young apprentices to do in our informal trade school."

"Okay." As they turned towards the basement door, she took Tom's hand. "We are supposed to see Dr. Beebee at the hospital tomorrow at eleven. It'll be our first ultrasound."

"Maria always liked those, though I don't know why."

"Really? I've been a little apprehensive, but if she liked them, I guess I can relax about it." She started down the stairs, and Tom followed. At the bottom, she said, "Let's look at the theater."

As they went in, Jenelle flipped the light switch. "I'm going to like our having this. What do you think about seating?"

"At first I thought in terms of recliners or overstuffed chairs from Montague's. Then an ad came to my personal email from an outfit that sells nothing but home theater furniture, lighting, and accessories. You should see their web site. It has ideas I'd never considered."

They sat down on an old love seat. Jenelle looked at him asking, "For instance?"

"We could put one or two sofas up on the back row, then wide recliners in the middle row, and overstuffed chairs in front – rather than just rows of reclining seats."

"Interesting! I like the idea of sharing a recliner with you!" Jenelle poked him.

"Another idea is theater furniture with provisions for holding snacks and drinks, like some theaters do." Jenelle nodded as he continued. "Have you thought about having a small snack station just outside the door, for cold drinks, hot drinks, or popcorn?"

"We've got to have popcorn. ... Are you hoping for a boy ... or a girl?"

He grinned. "Yes! Or both!"

Jenelle smiled. "You know that it's going to be hard to maintain my figure after this."

Tom looked into her eyes. "I'm not worried about that. We know each other very well, and I know you'll keep physically fit, just as I will, even into our old age."

"I'm looking forward to growing old with you, Tom."

He looked at her. "Even with wrinkles and white hair, I'm sure you'll still be amazing!" He paused. "How about we go upstairs, take a shower, and go to bed early?"

"You're on!" They got up and left the little theater. "I'm glad Paul suggested we have a spare bedroom down here. It'll be nice if, on a cold winter evening, we can come down here, see a movie, use the hot tub, and then go straight to bed. I'm going to put sheets on that bed tomorrow, and put some more towels in that bathroom."

14.

In the Hen the next morning, Tom and Jenelle were finishing their breakfast. Tom looked at his watch. "Paul will be at the station in about fifteen minutes."

"Okay." Jenelle waved at Effie to come over. "Effie, put this on our tab with your twenty, okay?"

"Sure thing, Jenelle. Coming back for lunch?"

"Unless something comes up. Tom is taking me to get my first ultrasound with Dr. Beebee this morning. I don't think I'll be late, though."

"Okay. If you aren't here by noon, shall I tell the church ladies why you're late?"

Jenelle nodded and smiled. "Sure! It's no secret!"

Jenelle and Tom went out the door and down the street to the station. It was already getting warm. The weather forecast was for another hot summer day with no rain in sight.

Going into the station, they were met with the cooler air of the air conditioning. Charly greeted them. "Good morning, Jenelle, Chief."

"Good morning Charly," Jenelle smiled.

Tom nodded. "I expected you to be home asleep by now. Weren't you on duty last night?"

"Yeah. I just came in to tell you that the library was vandalized last night. I took pictures and put them on your desk, Chief. I sent off some prints and cast of a footprint to the lab. It's mostly just a big mess to clean up, with books and magazines scattered on the floor, but a couple of computers were stolen. There were at least two. They got past the perimeter alarm, but when they tried to break into the office and work area, the security service got a signal, and a bell went off. At that point, they evidently ran. I called Ruth, and she came over at about 3:30.

She looked around and said she'd make some calls. She'll give us a damage list later today. I closed up the broken glass area as best I could do with plastic, then I hung around until one of the assistant librarians Ruth called came in. Now I can go home and get some sleep."

Tom nodded. "Thanks, Charly. Go ahead. Go home." Charly left, and Paul came in. Good morning, Paul. Come on into my office."

"Good morning, Chief." He followed him, went into Tom's office, and sat down. "We've got only a couple of more days of work, and your basement will be finished."

"That's great." Tom smiled. "Jenelle and I are going to order some home theater furniture and a few other things. Those are small jobs. We'll call you if we need you. Now, what about our apprentice program? Everett Beam has finished the paperwork and filed it with Sacramento."

Paul nodded. "That's great! The problem now is, I need to find some work for our apprentices. Towne is not exactly experiencing a building boom."

Tom looked at his friend. "I've got a couple of ideas, maybe three."

Paul took a notebook out of his pocket. "Shoot."

"First, do you know Joan Craver? She's a realtor friend of Jenelle's."

"Sure."

"Joan told Jenelle one day that there was a minor upgrade which can be done at Jenelle and Mike's old house, which would greatly increase its value. Joan told Jenelle that it would probably not cost more than seven thousand, and it would increase the house's value by three times that. You know where the house is, don't you?"

Paul nodded. "I remember. I'll call Joan later. What else do you have?"

"The library was vandalized last night. I don't know the extent of the damage yet. Even if you're not involved in the repairs, the library needs to be brought up to code, and our mayor knows it. More than that, few people know that the library has an attic. It's not used much because accessibility is a problem, but that can be improved, and maybe the mayor can get the City Council to foot the cost of finishing that attic. If work areas can be put into the attic, and main level of the library would have quite a bit of increased floor space for the future. I don't think it'll require an architect, but you will be able to determine that."

Paul was writing rapidly in his notebook. "That sounds like a good project, perhaps two. Do you have anything else?"

Tom nodded. "It's something that will most likely require an architect and city funds. You've known the Mayor for a long time. Try gently floating the idea of a Towne History Museum to him. We know now that the area has even more history to it than we thought. It could start as a wing of the library building or perhaps of City Hall."

Paul grinned. "That's a challenge, but I know just how to pull his chain. I can make a museum happen, but it will take time." He got out of his chair. "I'll head to the library right now, and see how much damage there is. My Dad helped build that building." He shook Tom's hand. "Thanks! I'll see ya later."

"All right, Paul." They shook hands, and Paul quickly went through the outer office and on out. He went back to going through his mail. He found the email of the web site selling home theater furnishings, and he sent it to the printer behind Jenelle's desk.

At 10:45, Jenelle came to his office door. "Jack is here, so we can head out to the hospital."

Tom looked at his watch. "Wow! The morning is going fast. Let's go." They left the patrol car in front of the station and took their personal car to the hospital. Inside, a nurse took Jenelle to the examining room and helped her into a gown before having her lie on the bed.

Dr. Chuck Beebee was a very friendly and easy-going guy. "You may feel a little uncomfortable with this, Jenelle, but it's not painful." He raised the head of the bed a little more, and he brought the ultrasound equipment over next to the bed. While Tom and Jenelle watched, Dr. Beebee put ultrasound gel on her stomach and began moving the transducer over her belly. They all kept their eyes on the screen. "Now, here we see your uterus, and you have more than one fetus." He continued to move the transducer around. "Yes! Here's one, ... a second one, ... a third one – you're going to have triplets, Jenelle!"

"Wow! This is incredible! Isn't it, Tom?"

Tom's grin was wide. "Fantastic!"

The doctor put on some more gel, and put the transducer back where it was. He adjusted a control on the machine. "We cannot positively determine sex yet, but I think at least one of them is a boy – but don't hold me to that at this point."

Tom's mouth was slightly open. "Triplets! It's a good thing we finished the basement! Now I'll have to child-proof the house again!"

Jenelle winked at him. "We're also going to need some child gates! When are we due? About Easter?"

Chuck Beebee nodded. "That sounds about right. As your pregnancy goes along, we'll narrow it down. Our next ultrasound should be in your second trimester." He backed the machine away. "Go ahead and get dressed again. I'll be back in a few minutes to talk about your next appointment."

+ + +

The news of Jenelle being pregnant with triplets spread around Towne fast. Friday morning, the Police Station phone lines were lit up almost constantly, and Jenelle was enjoying herself. At 10:30, a call came in for Tom, and she simply called out, "Line 2 for you, Tom."

He picked up the handset. "This is Police Chief Tom Kuster. How may I help you?"

"Mr. Kuster, this is Vatican City, please hold the line for the Bishop of Rome."

Tom sat up straight in his chair. "Jenelle!" He beckoned with a big gesture, with his eyebrows raised, for her to come into the office. She ended her call and came rapidly. As she came through the door, he said, "Jack's out there, so close the door." He put the speaker phone on.

"Mister Kuster, this is Pope Francis." Jenelle's eyes grew wide.

"Good morning, sir." Tom smiled.

"Good morning to you as well. I am calling about your discovery of a previously unknown mission site, and a journal by Francisco Palóu."

"Yes. To be completely accurate, the cave was discovered by my fourteen-year-old son, who is since deceased. He never saw the interior of the cave. On the same shelf as the journal was a two-volume version of the Bible in Latin and a Native American reader."

"Thank you for the clarification. We are excited here in Rome and elsewhere as a result of this discovery."

"That is understandable." Tom nodded. "We do not know how much information has reached you about it at this point."

"I understand. If you have the time, would you mind telling me some of the things that have happened since your son's discovery?"

"Certainly. My second wife is here in my office with me, and she and I will answer your questions as best as we can. Jenelle?" He nodded to her.

She cleared her throat. "After his entire family and my husband were killed in a train wreck, Tom shared with me the secret that he had shared with my first husband when they explored the cave. At the beginning, the opening into the cave was very small, and we depended upon battery-powered lights."

Tom continued. "Mike, her first husband, and I found a crude chapel behind a masonry wall in the main cave, with a cross on the wall, and the books on nearby shelving. In another part of the chapel, we found the remains of a priest on a small platform under a blanket. A doorway into an adjacent room led to a bathing area with fresh water, along with masonry stairs leading to other levels."

"Yes," said Jenelle, "We hired a couple of well-known archeologists, Leonard and Dava Cuchins, to examine the area more fully. We now have a full report from them, accompanied by more than a thousand images."

"Wonderful! This is simply marvelous. May I ask a favor of you?"

Tom looked at Jenelle, and they both nodded. Tom asked, "Are you wanting us to let a papal representative visit the site?"

A chuckle was heard from Rome. "Yes. Would that be possible?"

Tom was firm. "The cave is too small and fragile for a large delegation. We could escort one or two people into the site. It is not going to be a tourist attraction. They will have to wear casual clothing that can get dirty."

"That is very understandable. I will ask Cardinal Medina in San Francisco to call you and make arrangements. Thank you for your time. Are the two of you followers of our Lord Jesus Christ?"

"Yes, sir. We both attend Towne Community Church, which is an evangelical congregation."

"Very good. Thank you again for your time. May God bless you both."

"Thank you." They both said. The connection ended.

Jenelle stood up and went to the window. "That was amazing."

"Yes it was." He paused. "This coming visit presses us into doing something we should have done before."

She turned. "What's that?"

"We need to create an erosion-resistant path up the hill from the generator to the opening."

"Yes! You're right! We should have done this before! Who can we get?"

"You're still fielding calls about the triplets, so I'll call Pappy Hayes. He's retired and won't do it himself, but he'll know who to call."

Jenelle nodded and headed for the door. "Pappy will know who can do it. Even retired he's the best landscape architect within a hundred miles." She opened the door and went out.

The call was an easy one. Tom described the situation, and Pappy said he would send his son out to look things over, organize a work crew, and get it done. He said it might take two weeks at most.

As Tom hung up, Jenelle called out, "Paul for you on line two."

Tom picked it up. "Good morning, Paul. What's up?"

"Good morning, Tom. Dave just finished the installation of the video and sound equipment. Gary Pope and Jody Hickman finished the painting about an hour ago. They've done terrific work, above and beyond. You may want to pay them something a little extra. They're getting married soon. The basement's done except for placement of the furniture you ordered."

Tom leaned back in his chair. "Great! We also ordered a popcorn machine, a fridge for drinks, and a machine for making coffee, tea, and hot chocolate. When do you think the furnishings and other stuff will get here?"

Paul hesitated. "I haven't checked with the freight depot today, but as of yesterday I was told that they will hold it until all of it is there. They said they would deliver the whole load either Thursday or Friday of next week."

"How's the mayor's project coming?"

"Great! Work starts any day now. It'll be behind the library, with its own entrance on the other street, but there'll be a hallway connecting the two buildings. By the way, Dave says that Julie, his apprentice, will take her exams soon, and Dave plans to hire her. She's really good."

Tom sat up. "That's great, Paul. How soon are you sending me a final invoice for the basement?"

"I'll do it as soon as I get the final inspection."

"Great. Talk to you soon."

"Yeah, soon." Paul hung up.

Tom got up from his desk and went out to the main station office. Jody looked up. "Did you talk to Pappy?"

"Yeah, his son will see that it's done within a couple of weeks. I talked to Paul. The basement's done except for final inspection, and our furnishings delivery will be next week. He also said that Dave is getting ready to hire Julie, his apprentice, as soon as she passes her exams."

Jenelle nodded. "Julie's really sharp. How old do you think she is, twenty-two or three?"

Tom nodded. "She may be twenty-five, but don't tell I said that!"

Jenelle grinncd. "Right! I talked to Judy a minute ago about the museum project. She says we'll probably see in the paper tomorrow that the mayor plans to put a tax levy on the ballot to cover both the museum and the upgrades to the library. She said that with all the publicity about the mission, the levy should pass easily. It won't be an expensive one."

+ + +

Three weeks later, Tom stopped their car by the generator, and Cardinal Joseph Medina and his aide, Mario Sanchez, got out of the back seat. Tom took out a key and turned a key switch just above the generator enclosure's gate. The generator began its steady hum. Jenelle beckoned. "Follow me. The mission is right up this path." The two from San Francisco followed her, and Tom brought up the rear.

At the entrance, Jenelle took out her cell phone and dialed a number. "This is Jenelle Kuster at the Francisco Palóu mission. Code 15-12-3." Putting her phone away, she unlocked the gate and led them in.

Coming out of the conduit tunneled into the main cave, Cardinal Medina and Mario stood there in stunned silence, looking around. The Cardinal's voice was animated. "How long was all of this sealed up?"

Tom's voice was low out of habit. "As best as our archeologists can determine, the exact year of the slide is unknown, though it was probably the one recorded in nearby newspapers in 1811. The last entry in the journal of Francisco Palóu was for January 13, 1788. Since the church knows when and where Palóu was buried, the remains in the chapel were definitely not his." He paused. "This way to the chapel." He walked across to the little doorway. Tom turned on his hand-held floodlight, and led the way into the chapel.

Jenelle pointed her flashlight to the left. "There was a priest's remains on that little platform, under a blanket. Towne's Coroner autopsied the remains, and the analysis reported from the lab are in the archaeologists' report."

Tom nodded. "Before you leave, we will give you a digital copy of the report." He pointed towards the bathing pool. "There's a spring that constantly fills this pool, keeping the water fresh. The overflow ends up in the lake below us."

"Amazing!" Cardinal Medina knelt down, scooped some of the water from the pool with his hands, and drank. Mario Sanchez knelt beside him and did the same. As they stood up, Cardinal Medina walked towards the stairs and looked up. "May we go up?"

Jenelle shook her head. "I'm sorry, sir, the Cuchins say that the area is too fragile for visitors."

He nodded. "I understand." Turning back and into the chapel, he went to the altar, with Mario following. As they knelt at the altar, Jenelle and Tom could hear them quietly praying. As they stood up, the Cardinal turned to Tom and Jenelle. "We are fervently searching church historical records, trying to determine the identity of the priest that evidently died here. We may never know, of course."

Tom shook his head. "You may be right, but with God's help, someone may someday figure it out."

The cardinal nodded. "Yes, with divine help we may find the evidence. Thank you both for allowing us to see this. We have taken enough of your time."

Jenelle smiled. "It has been our pleasure." She led the way out.

Epilogue

The months that followed flew by quickly for Jenelle and Tom. They spent Thanksgiving with Mike and Tricia in San Francisco. While they were there, they sat down with people from both Community Evangelical Church and the Archdiocese of San Francisco. Cardinal Medina was there, and they talked about the mission cave, the Towne history museum, and the possibility of planting a Roman Catholic church in Towne.

Six graduate archeology students from UCLA came with their professor to examine the cave during their Christmas break. They were able to identify the Native American tribe that made the cross above the altar in the chapel.

The week after Christmas, at a baby shower for Jenelle, Jody Pope announced that she and Gary were going to have a baby sometime the following summer. On Valentine's day, Jack proposed to Dannie, and to his great surprise, she said yes. In church, they announced their plans to be married in June.

A week before Easter, Tom and Jenelle's Towne acquired three new residents. Jenelle gave birth to a boy and two girls. Jenelle insisted that they name them Tommie Michael Kuster, Alice Jenelle Kuster, and Karen Tricia Kuster.

Tom was more than okay with that.